P9-AGC-456

What If?

I Missed the Bus . . .

What If?

I Missed the Bus ...

by Jennifer Rabin

SCHOLASTIC INC.

New York   Toronto   London   Auckland   Sydney
Mexico City   New Delhi   Hong Kong

ISBN 0-439-08718-X

12 11 10 9 8 7 6 5 4 3 2 1   9/9 0 1 2 3 4/0

Printed in the U.S.A.   40

First Scholastic printing, June 1999

Chapter 1

Some people wake up with plenty of time to get ready for their day. My best friend, Lisa Williams, for example. She sets her alarm so she can lie in bed and wake up slowly — half in and half out of some dreamy cloudland — not that Lisa doesn't tend to visit cloudland even when she's not just waking up, but that's another story. So she has time for a nice, long bath — Lisa's into all kinds of essential oils and scented powders, to start her day balanced and happy. Time for a good mug of rise-and-shine tea.

Me, I guess I'm just not one of those good-morning-sunshine-type people. I hate waking up — maybe because I usually stay up too late practicing my guitar or reading the latest scare-you-wide-awake thriller in my favorite series. Whatever. Even when I do the early-to-bed thing, I can't get into the early-to-rise part.

That's why I've got my morning down to a

science. The Brittany Elliot don't-miss-a-minute-more-of-sleep-than-you-need-to science. 7:15: Alarm goes off. 7:16: Outta bed. 7:17–7:19: Make bed.

I'll spare you the nitty-gritty details. Suffice it to say that by 7:53, I've done it all and am walking out of the house with exactly enough time to catch the school bus two blocks away, at 7:58. So I'm not the first in line. So what? I make the bus.

Except that on this particular morning, my rhythm was off by a few minutes. 7:52: I slid my feet into my new red platform sneakers and tied them. 7:53: I pulled on my sweater. 7:53 and 30 seconds: I grabbed my loose-leaf binder off my desk and shoved it into my knapsack with all my other stuff.

And that's when I really hit a snag. See, one of the books in my bag wasn't mine, and I noticed it instantly. The cover was made out of this swirly lavender-pink-and-sunset-orange paper. Really beautiful handmade paper. The book was Lisa's diary, and she carried it almost everywhere.

Of course I'd seen it a zillion times, but I'd never read it. I mean, Lisa's my best friend. She's been my best friend for practically ever. But a diary's a diary. Besides, Lisa and I don't have any secrets. At least I didn't think we did. . . .

I eased the purple-and-pink-and-orange book out of my knapsack and stared at it. Well, Lisa *had* been going kind of weird on me lately. Looking at me kind of funny. Getting all quiet at things I said. Not returning my phone calls. I'd finally broached the subject over milk and mint sandwich cookies in my kitchen yesterday, and major spillage had ensued. By that I don't mean we knocked over our milk.

Like she said *I* was going weird on *her*. Making all kinds of comments. Excuse me? I always make comments. Lisa likes my comments. They make her laugh. Or used to. She's always thought it was great how I could cut straight to the chase. See right through people. Know what's real and what isn't. Or she *used* to think it was great.

Now, well . . . I wasn't sure exactly what was going on lately. I ran my finger over the soft, coarse, clothlike paper covering her diary. Maybe the answer was in here.

No. Uh-uh. *Back off, Brittany,* I told myself. I have a diary, too. A plain, basic black diary, like a closed door, and I'd kill anyone who read it. And anyway, I knew what would be in Lisa's diary. At least on the most recent page. At least I suspected I knew. Lisa probably would have written all about

3

"the big talk" in my kitchen. But what did she think, deep down, about it all?

See, I tend to wear my heart on my sleeve, as the expression goes — I say exactly what's on my mind. I don't hold back. But Lisa, well, she's more the quiet type. Still waters run deep and all that.

I'd come right out and said I thought Lisa was giving me the old brush-off — not calling me back, going all silent on me. But it had taken all kinds of prodding and coaxing to get her to say that she thought *I* was giving the brush-off to *her*. "I mean, why should I call you back," she'd asked, "when you don't want to do any of the things that are important to me?"

Oh, that. Then it started making a little more sense. Lisa had been bugging me, in her own special, quiet, persistent way, to pass out leaflets at school before homeroom about the pipeline they wanted to build in Bradford Harbor and all the incredibly gross sewage and garbage that would spew into the water.

I started wondering what she'd written about that in her diary. I could only imagine.

I shot a dirty look at the diary. I mean, please don't get me wrong. I'm all for a clean Bradford

Harbor. Totally. And I applaud Lisa's concern. It's part of the reason she's my best bud. She knows what's important. Lisa wants to save the whole world. But she kind of knows it too much sometimes. Like if she had her way, we'd be spending all — and I mean all — our free time healing the sick and talking to the dolphins — and Lisa would be down under the deep blue in her scuba gear at the very center of the discussion. She's the most generous person in the world and I love her for it, but sometimes she's just not the most practical.

I think that passing out leaflets is a waste of time. I know it's important to Lisa, but totally honestly? Totally, totally?

People like Liv and Carole and them were just going to throw those leaflets away. Liv and Carole were two of the "we're all that" girls at school. They'd only care if the pipeline was going to spew into J. Crew or The Body Shop.

I was getting angrier and angrier as I imagined what was in that perky, bright, swirly-covered diary. Why didn't Lisa realize that if she really wanted to do something, she should go down to the harbor and lie down on the beach so they couldn't get the bulldozers or the pieces of pipeline onto the sand.

But of course this really wasn't about the harbor, it was really about me and Lisa. Who respected whom. Who invited whom. Who called. Who cared. The "who's a more loyal friend" show.

After the milk-and-cookies talk, we kind of made up and I agreed to meet Lisa before homeroom and give out some leaflets. 'Cause it meant so much to her, and she's my closest friend.

Still, things hadn't been so smooth between us lately, and here I was in possession of her diary. A person could be excused for thinking it was fate that the diary ended up in my room right when Lisa had been acting so weird with me. Of course, I don't believe in fate. That's more Lisa's deal. The kind of thing she'd write about between her bright-colored diary covers.

Maybe we're just not meant to be friends anymore. Maybe fate has new friends in mind.

What if her diary said something like that? What if Lisa was on to the next person and yours truly was the last to know? Nah. Couldn't be. Lisa and I were a perfect pair. I mean, how many other thirteen-year-old girls actually agree with me that Dawson Leery is a total snore-bore? How many other girls my age would like to see Buffy the Vampire Slayer kick Dawson's wimpy, sensitive butt? Of course, Pacey is another matter. (Sigh.) Lisa and I agree on that, too.

But I'm getting off the subject. The point is, I was standing there with Lisa's diary in my hands. And something weird had been going on between us. Totally honestly? Totally, totally? I mean, what if I read it? Lisa wouldn't be any the wiser. What she didn't know couldn't hurt her. I'd just glance at the last few pages. Skim. See if there was anything I should know but didn't.

I took a deep breath and flipped open Lisa's diary. . . .

My name jumped out at me in Lisa's familiar round handwriting. I sank down on my bed and started reading.

Brittany was in rare form today. Such a . . . rhymes with witch! I wish she wouldn't be so hard on other people. She can be so critical.

I got that elevator-going-down feeling in the pit of my stomach. So much for that great way I could cut to the chase. It seemed Lisa would rather have a friend who just went around with a smiley face all the time, no matter what.

It's not that I don't get it — Brittany's obser-vations are killer. Gee, thanks, Lis. *But she alien-*

ates people. Right now, I'm feeling like one of them. I wonder what she really thinks about me?

I used to believe Lisa was honest. But was she really a two-faced so-and-so who wanted a sugar-coating?

Sarah and I were talking about her and Sarah was trying to help me decide what to do about the slumber party invitation I got. I closed my eyes. What slumber party? I hadn't been invited to any slumber party.

"Brittany! Hurry up!" That was my sister Charlee calling from downstairs. Charlee's taking a year off between high school and college and working as a teaching assistant. Getting life experience, she calls it. "You'll miss the bus! I'm leaving for work in two seconds, and I'm already late, so I can't drive you!"

I glanced at the clock. 7:56 and change. More than three minutes off. My pulse shot up. I slammed the diary closed. I'd read enough. More than enough. My pulse pounded. My chest felt tight. Stabbed in the back. Wounded. Furious. I tried to tell myself it was better this way. At least I knew what Lisa "Benedict Arnold" Williams really thought.

I shoved the diary back into my knapsack. I was outta there.

Chapter 2

I ran for the bus. My feet struck the pavement angrily. When had Lisa planned to let me in on the fact that only one of us thought we were still best friends? They say anger can give you an extra burst of speed. If this was the case, I should have been able to make the bus easily.

The problem was my new platform sneakers. The sneakers part sounds like you could really run in them. The platform part — well . . . they look good. Really good. But racing to where the school bus stopped was like trying to do a sprint with blocks strapped to the bottoms of my feet. I had to do this flat-footed kind of trot and be careful not to turn my ankle. When I put my shoes on this morning, I would have said I was willing to pay the price for beauty. But with Lisa's words pounding in my head, fab footwear hardly seemed like the most important thing in the world.

Meanwhile, it was pouring — one of those cold

October rains we get in New England — and I didn't have a second to go back for an umbrella. I kept running — trotting, whatever — my face wet, the rain dripping off the ends of my shoulder-length black hair. As I turned the corner, still a block away, I could easily see the bright yellow school bus, its doors open as it picked up passengers. Most of the kids who got on at my stop had boarded already, and as I went from trot to awkward canter, I could see the last person getting on.

"Wait! Wait!" I waved my arms and yelled. But the bus doors were closing. "No!" The bus pulled away, belching a cloud of exhaust out of its tailpipe.

I slowed down, out of breath. Darn it! It was barely 8:00 in the morning, and it was already one of those days when I absolutely should not have gotten out of bed. Not for a moment. A person who believed in fate could excuse this as my payback for snooping in Lisa's diary. But I don't believe in fate. Besides, how else was I supposed to find out what Lisa wouldn't come right out and say to my face? The hurt and fury flowed like punch at a pool party.

And now I was going to be late for school, on top of everything else. I started running again. Maybe I could catch the bus at the next stop. The rain and wind stung my face. I pumped my legs. My lungs burned. My ankles hurt from my platform-impaired stride.

The bus disappeared around the corner. I gave it my Jackie Joyner-Kersee. Go for the gold! Push for the finish line! I turned onto Caroline Street just in time to see a lone passenger getting on the bus at the last stop before school. I ran as hard as I could. I was almost there. But almost wasn't good enough.

I was just in time to get another lungful of exhaust as the bus started rolling. I came to a soggy stop. The thighs of my jeans were wet and clung to me like plastic wrap. My hair fell in soaked stringy strands. My best friend thought I rhymed with "witch."

I considered turning around and going home. Shedding my wet clothes, taking a hot bath, getting into some sweats, and canceling the rest of the day. I'd call Mom at work and tell her I was sick. I'd make myself a mug of steaming hot chocolate, and as I drank it, I'd tear out the pages of Lisa's diary and burn them one by one. I'd use the matches I'd snagged as a souvenir from the restaurant we'd gone to for her thirteenth-birthday brunch. The one where I'd been seated right next to her, in the friend-of-honor spot. I thought using those matches would be a nicely ironic touch.

HONK! SCREEEECH!! The blare of the bus horn and a metallic squeal of wet brakes shocked me out of my diary-burning daydream. My breath stuck in my throat as I saw the school bus fishtailing wildly at the end of the street. It veered off to the left. To the right, I saw the blur of two faraway figures, darting from the middle of the street to the safety of the sidewalk on the right side of the road. And then the bus was heading straight off the road, sliding, sliding, sliding . . . dead-on into a thick tree. I was vaguely aware of my own scream, mingling with the sick sound of shattering glass and crumpling metal.

Chapter 3

The front, right part of the bus was crushed around the tree. The windshield was missing a jagged piece of glass. But by the time I had raced over, my heart in my throat, I could see that people were walking around inside the bus and that the vehicle was intact, except for the area around the doors and the stairs. I heard one person crying softly, but it sounded more like relief than fear.

Mrs. Jackson's familiar face appeared out one of the side windows. Mrs. Jackson was the bus driver, a large woman with coffee-and-cream skin and a perfect record for getting her kids to school safely and on time. Until now.

"We need some help," she said to me.

I felt another jolt of fear. "Is anyone hurt?"

Mrs. Jackson shook her head. "Just a few bumps and scratches. We were lucky, lucky, lucky. But we'll need some assistance." Then she seemed to do a double take. "How'd *you* get out *there*, baby?" Mrs. Jackson called all the kids on her route "baby."

"I missed the bus," I said. "I didn't get on at my usual stop. I was running after you, trying to catch up. I guess you didn't see me."

"Well, I guess you caught up." Mrs. Jackson shook her head. "And here we are. Stuck. Of course, we could climb out the emergency exit, but with this rain, it makes more sense to stay put until help gets here."

Grasped by the terror of the accident, I'd been briefly oblivious to the weather. Now I was suddenly aware, all over again, of how hard the rain was coming down. Several cars had stopped at the curb. One of the drivers, an older man in a neat gray suit, got out and offered to call 911 on his car phone.

"Someone needs to check on those two kids, too," Mrs. Jackson added. She pointed across Caroline Street at the pair I'd seen darting from the road. "Baby, would you go see if they're all right?"

I nodded. Up closer, I could see that there was a little boy — around my sister Annie's age, maybe eight or nine — in a yellow rain slicker. With him was a girl in a shapeless beige raincoat. Wait. That looked like . . . Carnie Bryson. Carnage.

Carnage, as everyone called her behind her

back, was the girl you didn't want to get stuck with for a science partner. The girl you didn't want to sit near in class. The girl you crossed the street to avoid. I know that sounds harsh, but that is the way it was. And here I was, crossing the street *toward* her. I had to wonder what I was doing.

Carnage always looked like a total wreck. Her clothes were ancient. And I don't mean vintage. Hey, I've gotten some of my fave outfits at Secondhand Rose. Like my burgundy velvet vest and plum-colored satin jeans. But I'm getting off the subject. The point is, Carnage dressed in seriously used. Threadbare, stained. People said she smelled bad, too — a fact I hadn't gotten close enough to confirm, thank you. Carnage was always getting to school late, and I heard she cut classes and that her brother might be in jail. Whatever. The girl was scary.

I paused a few feet away from her. What was Carnage doing with that little boy? Had she led him out into the street without bothering to check if the road was clear?

She looked over at me, her pale, even-featured face showing no emotion. We'd gone to school together for three years, but she didn't give any indication that we knew each other.

"Um, are you okay?" I asked warily. I noticed that the little boy was crying. What had Carnage done to him?

"Well, we're not flattened beneath the bus, if that's what you mean," Carnage said. "But I think he may have hurt his arm."

Carnage had hurt the little boy? I closed the distance between him and me in a few fast strides. I knelt down in front of him. "What happened?" I asked gently.

The little boy's lip trembled. "The bus . . . I was crossing the street and I looked up and it was . . . coming right at me and, well, all of a sudden I couldn't move! I just stood there, and I would have been killed if . . . if . . . she hadn't . . ." His words trailed off in breathy sobs.

I looked up at Carnage. Realization hit like an early morning cold shower. "You mean, you . . . saved him!?" I asked in amazement.

"Surprise, surprise," Carnage muttered. She ran a hand through her short brown hair.

How embarrassed was I? My cheeks must have been as red as my new — and, I might add, thoroughly, hopelessly waterlogged — shoes. Carnage Bryson — excuse me, Carnie Bryson — was a hero. "Oh, my god, I'm sor — I mean, that's great, I mean . . . thanks, Carnie. It's really, really lucky you were here."

Carnie shrugged. "Yeah, whatever," she replied, a hard edge in her voice. I guess I couldn't blame her. I mean, what did I expect when I'd practically accused her of throwing the poor little kid in front of the bus. Was she supposed to jump up and hug me like I was her best friend? Wait. Scratch that. The term "best friend" was kind of an empty one for me this morning. What with supposed best friends writing nasty comments in their diaries. . . .

Meanwhile, the girl I'd vote least likely to save the day was stooping down next to me and talking sweetly and gently to the boy. "You're gonna be all right. Promise. Someone called for help. We'll get your mom. . . ." She turned to me. "The kid just froze or something when he saw that bus coming at him. I yanked him out of the way, but we both fell. I think he landed on his arm. Hey, champ, can you go like this? Can you bend your arm back and forth?" She flexed her arm at the elbow, her raincoat hanging on her as if it belonged to someone else.

The little boy's arm dangled at a weird angle. He

shook his head, his tears continuing to fall. Carnie bit her lip. "Hey," she said lightly. "You'll be okay. Besides, if it's broken, a cast looks way cool. I'll sign it."

I felt a tug of admiration. "I'll sign it, too," I told the little boy.

Carnie reached out and patted his head. "So, you know the one about the patient with the broken arm?" she asked. "Well, the doctor's putting the final wrapping on the cast, and he tells the patient he'll be good as new in a couple of months," Carnie said. "The patient asks, 'Doc, will I be able to play the piano?' And the doctor tells him, 'Sure.' Well, the patient gets this big, goofy grin on his face and he says, 'Gee, Doc, that's great, 'cause I couldn't play the piano before!'"

I kind of groaned and giggled. The little boy did, too, and it seemed to make him less frightened.

It just goes to show that you never know about people. I mean, Carnie was this softie in disguise — in addition to having saved the little boy from becoming roadkill in a yellow raincoat. Okay, okay, I know that's really not funny, but you have to use humor in these situations. And this morning definitely qualified as a situation. First Lisa and the diary. Then the accident. And now I'm actually standing in the pouring rain, with nothing but respect for Carnie Bryson! Well, rock my little world.

I heard the wail of approaching sirens — bending and shifting from low and faraway to high and shrill as they drew nearer quickly. A caravan of emergency vehicles squealed around the corner, lights flashing. They screeched up to the site of the accident. Police cars, fire trucks, EMS vehicles. Fortunately, the sum total of Bradford's emergency resources weren't really necessary here this morning. On the other hand, it was kind of exciting. Uniformed personnel jumped out and raced toward the bus.

But Carnie wasn't sticking around for the action. "They'll take care of you now," she said to the boy. "You were very brave, you know that?" And all of a sudden, she was on her feet and hurrying away.

"Carnie?" I called after her. What was up with the back door exit?

She paused just long enough to look over her shoulder at me. "Do me a favor," she said. It was more of an order than a request. "You don't know me, okay? You don't know my name. As far as you're concerned, I was never here."

I arched an eyebrow. I didn't understand. "Somehow they'll end up thinking it was my fault," Carnie

19

said. I opened my mouth to protest. "You thought that at first," she pointed out. I shut my mouth. She turned and hurried away.

I felt deeply, totally awful. I stuck around just long enough to make sure the little boy was safe and in good hands. One of the EMS attendants took charge of examining his arm, while her partner telephoned the boy's parents.

The kids on the bus were being taken out through the windows one by one and sheltered under big umbrellas by the emergency personnel until a backup bus arrived. If I'd made it to my stop on time, I would have been one of them. And I could still hitch a ride on the next bus they sent. But I was so wet already, I figured I might as well walk the rest of the way to school. I'd probably get there sooner, and I was late enough as it was. Besides, I had an ulterior motive.

I caught up with Carnie a couple of blocks away from school.

"That was an incredibly good deed you did," I said to Carnie as we headed through the rain toward school. "I would have told them you were Bradford's own personal Wonder Woman, if you'd

20

let me. I really would have. That little boy would have, too. I mean, you could have stuck around and bathed in the glory."

Carnie peered at me from under her umbrella. Several of the metal spokes were bent. "Funny you used the word 'bathed,'" she said flatly.

I felt my cheeks get as hot as a number-one single. Up close and personal, as they say, Carnie didn't smell and she wasn't dirty. Her coat was threadbare but clean. Maybe she was a bit hardened — older-looking than thirteen somehow. But I was beginning to understand why. "People can be so mean," I said sympathetically.

Carnie made this funny face — a sideways sneer with her mouth, but with a vulnerable, telltale moistness in her eyes. "Can you blame me for not wanting to stick around?" she asked. "Some of the kids on that bus are so . . . so . . ."

"So *Liv*?" I supplied. Liv Magnuson was queen of the "all that" crowd. All that brand-new, expensive clothing. All that smugness. All that attitude that said, *We're better than you.*

Carnie laughed. It was a little laugh, but it was the first time I'd seen her do that. Ever, I think.

"She of the perfectly shiny, perfectly blow-dried

hair," I said. "She would definitely not approve of my current drowned-rat look."

Carnie eyed me for a moment. "I suppose you can get under my umbrella, if you want," she said.

"I don't think I can get much wetter," I said. "But thanks."

Carnie and I walked along in silence for a block or so. "Listen, Carnie," I said. I took a deep breath. "I'm really, really sorry if I said anything that upset you back there. You saved that little boy's life, and *I* at least know it. You should be incredibly proud of yourself."

Carnie looked at me for a long moment. "Brittany, right?" I nodded. "Look, I know the stuff you've heard about me. I know what everyone in school says. It's not your fault you got the wrong impression."

I knew she was trying to let me off the hook, but I just felt worse. "Maybe it is my fault," I said. "I mean, I never tried to find out how it really is. And I'm sorry I didn't do it sooner, but I'm listening now. Okay?"

Carnie nodded slowly. "Okay," she said.

As we walked to school, she set the record straight. Her brother had been in trouble as a boy, it was true. But now he was grown-up and in the army. Not in jail. There was a new baby sister in the house, and Carnie's mother worked the night shift so she could care for the baby during the day. That was why Carnie was late for school a lot. She couldn't leave the baby until her mother got home from work. No, she didn't smoke and she never had. Did she cut classes? She admitted that the grapevine had gotten that one thing right. But honestly — could I blame her? I mean, I wouldn't want to go to school if people were that cruel and vicious to me.

I was getting the picture, and it wasn't a pretty one. Carnie didn't have any money for new clothes or going out for something to eat after school or to see the first-run movies everyone talked about. And because of that, people thought she was weird. They started rumors about her. And the rumors took hold. Lisa and I never openly humiliated her, the way some of the kids did. But we never defended her, either.

We rounded a curve, and the long, low, L-shaped building of Bradford Junior High loomed into view. I thought I saw Carnie square her shoulders, getting ready to sacrifice herself to the cruelties of eighth grade. Well, today I'd be right by her side when she went in there. Today she wasn't going to have to go it alone.

Was I being brave? Was I being noble? Well, I certainly didn't intend to abandon Carnie. Not after everything I'd learned this morning. I took a deep breath. Now, more than ever, I wished I'd never gotten out of bed today.

Chapter 4

I shed my sopping sweater and hung it in my locker. I pulled my wet hair off my face and tied it in a ponytail with an extra elastic band I kept with my gym stuff. But most of all, I tried to ignore the comments around me. "Look at her," I heard someone say. "Look at her hair and clothes. Eew, what a mess!" That sounded like Jane Bonner, one of Liv's ladies-in-waiting.

"She even smells a little like Carnage. Did you notice when she walked by us, Jane?" And that would be Carole Johannsen. Carole had added the *e* to the end of her name at the beginning of junior high. Like that dumb *e* made her more glamorous or something. Jane didn't need a fancy name to be glamorous. With her delicate features, long, straight flaxen-blond hair, and up-to-the second clothes that she and her mother got on weekend shopping trips to Boston, she was plenty glamorous all on her own.

I sneaked a look. Sure enough, Carole and Jane were standing by their lockers, giggling and staring at me, and making faces as if they'd tasted a rotten egg.

"Ole Carnage finally found herself a friend," Carole said nastily, tossing her strawberry-blond hair.

"Yeah, ole Spittany," Jane cracked. They both laughed as if it were the funniest thing on the planet.

Nearby, Carnie put her coat and umbrella in her locker. Her face showed no emotion, but there was no way she could be missing this.

We'd been a two-person parade from the second we'd passed through the entrance to school. People whispering, sneaking sidelong glances, making me feel as if I had breakfast dribbling from my mouth or I'd sprouted crabgrass instead of hair. This was how it was for Carnie every day. This was how it had been for three excruciating years.

I slammed my locker sharply, angrily, the metallic sound echoing in the hall.

"Hey, Lisa, looks like you've been dumped for Carnage Bryson!" I heard Carole call out.

Lisa! I spun around. She stood a few feet away, her mouth tight. I stared back, my pulse racing.

"So much for a clean harbor," she said stiffly.

Oh, that. With everything that had happened this morning, those leaflets just weren't the first thing on my mind. "Lisa, I was late because —"

"— you always leave everything till the last second," she finished. "How many extra minutes did you get to sleep this morning? Three? Four? Five really, really important minutes?" Lisa didn't get angry easily, but she was angry now.

"There's an explanation."

Lisa frowned. "There's always an explanation."

Anger pounded in my ears. Every muscle was as tight as a rubber band slingshot. *She* was mad at *me*? Miss Secretly Rhymes with Witch was putting *me* on the spot? "Okay, you don't want to hear it? Fine," I said.

"Well, if it's fine with you, it's fine with me," she said in a small voice. She sneaked a look over at Carnie. Then back at me. "What's happening to you?" she asked. She let out a breath like a deflating balloon and walked away.

I looked over at Carnie, too. She shut her locker and gave the combination dial a spin. "Welcome to my world," she said grimly. "I'm sorry."

I gave my head a hard shake. "Well, I'm not," I told her. "At least I know the truth about some people." I could only hope against hope that "at least" would provide a little consolation.

It wasn't until after Lisa slunk off that I remembered I still had her diary in my knapsack.

The "survivors" from the bus accident showed up shortly after we did. Yeah, that's what everyone was calling them. "The survivors." As if they'd weathered the Storm of the Century out on the high seas. Which was just about the size of the story by the time it finished spreading around school: Like it was a miracle the kids on the bus were alive. Like a monster oil tank truck had cut them off, and they'd almost blown sky-high — every last one of them. Or like they'd barely missed crashing into the house on the corner and obliterating a family of five inside. Or like Mrs. Jackson had passed out at the wheel, and some new kid had jumped into the driver's seat just in the nick of time.

Frankly, I didn't see a hair out of place on Liv's perfectly coiffed head. I was the one who looked as if I'd taken a storm-tossed dip on the way to school — new shoes and all. But Liv was milking the occasion for all the attention she could get. Carnie and I stood off to one side of the crowd as Liv held court with Carole and Jane and Natalia

Lopez. Half the Bradford Junior High football team clambered around them. I could hear Liv regaling everyone with her near-death experience.

"You think before the bus hit the tree, she saw her wardrobe flash before her eyes?" Carnie asked bitterly.

"Nah, her wardrobe's too big. She wouldn't have had time for that," I said. "Maybe just the pants."

But Liv's fans and admirers bought it all. "It is just, like, so cool that you made it through," Josh DeBeers was saying. Josh had this sun-kissed, surfer thing going, and I'd been secretly crushing on him for a few weeks in seventh grade. Now, hanging around Liv like a devoted puppy, he seemed so unworthy of a moment's heartache.

Liv wasn't paying much attention to him, either. I saw her wave at a boy standing on the edge of the crowd. I'd never seen him before. Believe me, if I had, I would have remembered it. Wavy, sandy-colored hair and a smattering of freckles across the bridge of his nose, with full lips and deep-set eyes, and . . . well, let's just say the sum of his parts added up to serious crush material.

He waved back at Liv — a little wave, kind of shy, I thought, and he smiled this really cute, lopsided smile. With a dimple and everything. So there really was a new boy in school — that much the rumor mill had actually gotten right.

But as soon as I got over my initial stupor at his cuteness, I felt a cold blast of envy and frustration. Who was I to think he'd ever turn that smile on me? There was her Liv-ness, waving him over to join her special little world. And here I was, my hair dripping, my clothes droopy, standing with the biggest reject in the school. I really don't mean anything against Carnie by that. I learned way better this morning. What I'm trying to get at is that just because I was associating with her, I was now the second biggest reject in the school.

Carnie and I scored our late passes as if we'd been on the bus with the "survivors." "It's the only way to avoid getting marked down for a demerit," Carnie said. If you got too many demerits, you got lunchtime detention.

So we slipped into the Torpedo's office in the middle of the pack. The Torpedo is our principal, Ms. Torpe. She whips her icy-blond helmet of hair into submission with an arsenal of sprays and gels and wears these wrinkle-free, sensible suits. The net effect is a little frightening. So you can imagine that

I was holding my breath as she issued my pass. But there were so many kids in the office, she barely looked up. "Brittany Elliot," she wrote. She didn't ask any questions.

Carnie and I took our passes and beat a hasty retreat out of Torpedo range.

At that moment, I noticed Liv standing nearby, watching us. Natalia and that cute new boy were with her. "Liars," Liv hissed at us. "No way you were on the bus. We would have smelled you."

I flinched. I felt as if I'd taken a sucker punch to the stomach. The new guy was staring at us. My face got hot with shame. I forced myself to stare back at him. I wasn't going to let him get to me. He lowered his gaze.

"Come on, Carnie," I said. I grabbed her arm.

"What's up with them?" I heard the new boy ask as we brushed past them.

"You don't want to know," Liv answered. "Does he, Natalia?"

"You definitely don't, Jack," Natalia answered.

Jack. The new boy was named Jack. And to judge by his company, he was just as shallow and phony as the rest of that crowd.

"You know, I thought . . . well, never mind," I heard him say as we left the office.

Chapter 5

By the time science was over, my new nickname seemed to be official. "Hey, Spittany!" I heard some random boy call out. I looked around but I wasn't sure who in the crowded hall was jeering at me. But as soon as I started walking, I heard another voice. "Yo, Spittany and Carnage," someone else guffawed.

I tried to play it as if it didn't bother me in the slightest. Emphasis on "as if." "Gee," I said loudly to Carnie. "Everyone knows who we are. We're famous."

Then there it was again, scrawled across the front of my locker in black Magic Marker. S-P-I-T-tany!!! Jeez, had they broadcast it over the loudspeaker or something? "Oh, someone went to the trouble to personalize my locker," I said brightly. "How nice is that?"

In Spanish class, Natalia Lopez made a calculated show of choosing the seat farthest away from me — and conveniently close to the new boy, Jack. "Does someone want to crack a window a bit?" she asked, eyeing me in the most obvious way.

"Why? Did you eat beans for breakfast?" I asked with patently put-on innocence. And I have to say, I was immensely gratified to see that Jack guy stifle a chuckle. Maybe he wasn't quite as awful as I thought.

But totally honestly? Totally, totally? The snappy retorts got tired, fast. By the time lunch rolled around, sitting in the cafeteria and fielding verbal potshots was about as appealing as the Muzak in my dentist's office.

Carnie and I took our time getting to the lunch-room. Notice I didn't say our sweet time, because knowing what lay ahead of us was anything but sweet. The lunchroom was a study in real-life social anthropology — and Carnie and I were at the bottom of the totem pole. I peered through the window on one of the heavy swinging doors, but I didn't go in.

"All in their places, with bright shiny faces," I commented to Carnie. By that I meant Liv and company, at their usual table by the back door —

the table everyone knew was reserved for the jocks and kings and queens of Bradford J.H.S. I could see that the new guy was sitting with them.

The assorted misfits and losers sat closest to the kitchen. Leon Lurie — math genius but just about unable to do anything in the real world, like tie his own shoes, for example. Jen Rebozo — picks her nose in public, 24/7. Neil Aggerman — just basically the biggest nerd this side of the Atlantic. Maybe on the other side, too. That was the table with Carnie's invisible place card. And now there was another one next to it that said S-P-I-T-tany!!!

But the table I cared about most — the one that drew my attention and kept it — was the unglamorous but perfectly okay table where Lisa and I usually ate lunch. I felt a deep twinge of unhappiness as I saw she was already there. With Sarah. She of the diary fame. Lisa's new adviser and chief counsel on slumber party invitations and ex-friends who rhymed with witch.

I saw Lisa pull a stack of her leaflets out of the Guatemalan woven shoulder bag she carried her books in. Sarah slid over close to her. I bit my lip. Sarah was the good friend. Sarah was the one concerned with saving the harbor and yacking it up with the dolphins. I felt a tickle of jealousy. Followed by anger. I took two giant steps away from the door.

Carnie studied me. "Wanna cut out of here?" she proposed.

My stomach did this nervous somersault. "You mean leave school? Sneak out?" It was totally against the rules.

Carnie gave a wordless shrug. I guess the rules hadn't helped her any.

I took another look into the cafeteria — at Lisa's red hair next to Sarah's light brown ponytail as they bent their heads together.

"I'll follow you to the nearest exit," I said to Carnie.

Confession: It was fun breaking the rules and sneaking out of school in the middle of the day.

Carnie had our jailbreak worked out as smoothly as butterscotch pudding. She chose a spot just down the hall from the front entrance — out of the security guard's vision, but where he could easily hear her. She planted herself like a football player getting set for a play. "Get ready," she whispered to me. She let loose a shrill scream.

We heard the squeak of the guard's chair against

the linoleum, and a second later, he came zooming around the corner in his gray uniform.

"Down there!" Carnie said, sounding urgent as she pointed toward the end of the hall.

As soon as the guard took off, she grabbed my sleeve. Holding back a burst of giggles, we made a break for it. Around the corner, past the empty security desk, and out the front doors to freedom. The rain was still coming down, but this time I got under Carnie's umbrella with her immediately. As we walked across the soft, soggy school lawn, our laughter met the sound of the rain.

"Oh, wow, I feel like Claire Danes in *Mod Squad!*" I gasped.

"Good thing it worked," Carnie said. "It's usually a lot simpler. The guard who's normally there — well, she's all addicted to those daytime soaps. She has this tiny little portable TV she plugs in at lunchtime, and I swear, the whole school could be kidnapped by Martians and she'd never notice."

Frankly, I could think of a growing list of kids who I wouldn't miss for a little green moment if they were suddenly, mysteriously to disappear. I was happy to leave them behind for the great, glassed-in comfort of the Bradford Plaza Mall. I felt giddy, emancipated. I made my own rules. Hear me roar.

And okay, so maybe the mall isn't the most exciting place in the world. But it's that forbidden fruit deal I was talking about before. The fact that we weren't supposed to be there somehow made it all the more exciting that we were. I mean, take your basic chocolate ice-cream cone. Good at just about any hour — I mean, if you're a chocoholic like me, at least. But for breakfast? When nobody's looking? Indescribably, incredibly delicious.

What I'm trying to say is I've clocked plenty of time at the mall. I mean, what kid in Bradford hasn't? But I'd never been here on a school day at lunchtime. At least not since I was a toddler holding onto my mother's hand. I took it all in as Carnie and I walked around.

People my age were conspicuously missing, though a group of high school kids were doing up some submarine sandwiches at the food court and trying to see who could blow their straw wrapper the farthest. There was a healthy contingent of grown-ups who looked to be on their lunch break, making the rounds at the stores and parting with all the money they'd earned since breakfast. One woman had no less than five different shopping bags — I counted them. There were moms with their babies, and the occasional cool, role-model dad with his. A posse of senior citizens was power-walking lap after lap around the inside atrium. They were definitely the group in charge on a midweek day.

Me and Carnie? We experimented with the tester lipsticks at the Face. We went into Tower Records and listened to a whole bunch of songs at the listening stations. We thumbed a bio of Seth Green until the bookstore clerk shot us dirty looks.

We weren't Carnage and Spittany. We weren't hopeless outcasts. We were just two girls hanging out at the mall. Two girls cool enough to know when to bend the rules a little. We wound up at the tables and chairs by the indoor fountain. The rain came down on the oversized, pyramid-shaped sky-light above us. Somehow, the Bradford Plaza Mall felt like an adventure today.

Carnie put her brown-bag lunch on the table — a pb and j sandwich, a carton of chocolate milk, a little container of Jell-O, and one of those plastic sleeves with a spork, a plastic knife, and a napkin, that she'd swiped from the cafeteria. She offered to share with me, but I had my eye on a ham and cheese on a croissant from the sandwich cart. It was a splurge but, hey, I was making the rules for this one little hour in my day, wasn't I?

"Can you put an extra piece of cheddar on it?" I asked the woman behind the cart, just because I could. I watched her fix the sandwich. For a day that had started as a dark blot on my calendar, I was feeling pretty good. The woman spread a layer of shredded lettuce on top of the ham and cheese, added a slice of tomato, and put the top half of the croissant back on. She speared her creation with a toothpick decorated with a French flag. As if. Tell me the French really slice their croissants and stuff them with American sandwich ingredients. But I was perfectly happy with my U.S. sandwich on a French roll.

The woman put it on a paper plate. "That'll be four twenty-five," she said. I dug into my baby-sitting money and paid her.

"Thank you. Have a nice day."

"You know, I think I actually will," I said. I took my lunch and turned to go. And found myself face-to-face with the Torpedo.

Chapter 6

I got off because it was my first offense. Also because Carnie took the heat for me — Carnie, whose real name I'd never used until today. It would have been too easy for her to run when she saw I'd been Torpedoed. I mean, all she had to do was sneak away from the table and make a break for it. It would have been way simpler than getting past the guard at school. But Carnie walked right up to the Torpedo and told her that our trip to the mall was her idea. So I was off, while Carnie pulled lunchtime detention every day for a week.

"You didn't have to do that for me," I said later, when the Torpedo was finished firing at us. Carnie and I beat it out of her office for the second time that day and headed for our lockers.

"Hey, we were in it together, weren't we?" she said, as if it were no big deal. "I mean, we're friends, right?" she added less certainly.

"Of course, right," I said firmly. I mean, if there

was a test for friendship and loyalty, Carnie had just passed it.

"Besides, I'm used to getting in trouble, and you're not," she said with a shrug. "Look at it this way. I won't have to eat in the cafeteria."

Our misadventure spread all over school like butter on warm toast. You have to wonder how these things get around. I mean, I certainly hadn't told anyone. Who was I going to tell? Lisa? We weren't even on speaking terms. And who was Carnie going to tell? But by midafternoon, I think the flies in the kitchen knew.

I was a little nervous about facing Lisa in English class. I mean, on the one hand, I kept telling myself I shouldn't care what my traitor of an ex-best friend thought. On the other hand, of course I cared. I'd shared every secret in my life with Lisa. No matter how angry with her I was, I couldn't wave some invisible wand and make her opinion not matter all of a sudden.

The second I saw her sitting there in class, purposely not looking up as I came into the room, I felt this tugging in my chest. My feet seemed to have a mind of their own. Before I'd thought it out, I was walking over to her.

"You know, half of why I got in trouble was because of you," I blurted out. Kids filed in around us and took their seats. I knew they were staring.

Lisa looked up. There was hurt in her brown eyes. "Excuse me?" she asked in a small, tight voice. "Correct me if I'm dreaming, but I wasn't the one who cut out of school. I wasn't the one playing hooky in the mall. I don't get it, Brittany. I mean . . . since when did you decide you looked up to . . . Carnie Bryson?" She dropped her voice to a whisper, as if Carnie were the name of some unspeakable disease.

My anger flared. "At least I know who my friends are . . . and aren't!" I shrugged off my knapsack, yanked it open, reached in for Lisa's diary, and hurled it at her desk. "Go to your stupid sleepover . . . without a certain person who rhymes with witch!"

Lisa's eyes opened wide with shock. "You . . . read my diary?!" She grabbed it and hugged it to her chest.

Everyone in class was tuned in to the Brit and Lisa show, but I was in way too deep to care. "I wanted to know what my supposed best friend thought of me," I thundered. "And now I do!"

"And now the rest of us do, too," said a new voice. I felt my face blaze as Ms. Halvorson, our

42

teacher, strode over to us from the front of the room. "If you'd like to hold it until after class, we've got an appointment here with a Mr. Charles Dickens. I think he'll provide you with plenty of drama and excitement, if that's what you're looking for."

I quickly took my seat and tried to focus my attention on *Great Expectations*. Ms. Halvorson wasn't kidding about the drama and excitement in that book. Convicts, criminals, crazy old ladies in ancient, tattered wedding dresses . . . Normally, English was my best subject. But today, I barely heard a word of the discussion. Oh, I was busy being studious, all right. Studious about avoiding Lisa's hurt, angry gaze.

I was outta there as soon as the bell rang. I gathered up my books and stuffed them back into my knapsack — minus the diary — and bolted like a steel door lock. I couldn't help noticing that Lisa didn't even try to catch up with me.

It was war on the girls' side of the gym. The dodgeball flew back and forth across the high-ceilinged room like cannon fire, accompanied by shouts and clapping and the periodic squeak of rubber-soled gym shoes on the polyurethaned wood floor. Now most people will tell you that dodgeball's not a real sport. That it's for wimps. I mean, you don't see it being played on TV on the *X-treme Zone*. And you won't see superbly conditioned Olympic athletes hurling a dodgeball at one another for the pride of team and country. But the way we played it at Bradford Junior High, it was serious stuff.

It started even before the first ball was thrown. See, the whole eighth grade has gym at the same time — girls on one side of the wall divider, boys on the other. We all pile into the locker room and put on our gym suits. And wow, that's a real fashion leveler — that is to say, everybody looks pretty much equally bad in a gym suit.

Okay, so Jane Bonner wears hers with her tiny, diamond-stud earrings and top-of-the-line Nike tennis shoes. And Carnie wears hers with worn-out Skippies. But a gym suit is a gym suit. It's a baggy, ugly, idiotic item of clothing, and we'd all be much happier in a simple pair of navy gym shorts and a T-shirt.

The point is, wearing the same awful thing makes all of us just a little more equal than usual. Which causes some people to play especially hard and viciously to gain back their advantage. Or other people to play especially hard and viciously to get even for being on the bottom the rest of the day.

We piled out of the locker room and into the gym in our navy-blue suits. Lisa and I were giving each other the old freeze-out, and I have to admit it felt deeply bad. I was talking to Carnie and pointedly ignoring everyone else. And Lisa was talking and laughing with Sarah P.

Ms. Anteles, standing at ground zero in the center of the gym, gave a shrill blast on her whistle. It echoed off the walls. Ms. Anteles is short and compact, but every inch of her is steel-hard muscle. She wears black lace-up combat boots, camouflage shorts, and a Navy Seal cap over her spiky blond hair. You won't catch her in something as laughable as a gym suit. We fell completely silent at the whistle.

"Listen up, people!" she roared. "The name of the game is dodgeball. No hits above the shoulders. Everything else goes. You get hit, you're out of the game. Winner is the team with the last woman standing. Choosing up sides — Hoffman, over there, O'Rourke, other side."

Lynn Hoffman and Samantha O'Rourke took their stands on opposite ends of the gym, and each chose the first girl for her team. The popular girls were chosen first, along with the good athletes, like Val Washington (starting center of the girls' basketball team) and Jeannie Pirandello (Massachusetts's junior all-around track star). Me, I'm not bad at dodgeball, and I usually get chosen pretty early on.

But today, I stood around with the shrinking group of last picks, old Spittany, trying to pretend that it didn't matter.

I watched Lisa get chosen by Lynn's team, a few dozen picks after Liv and Jane. When it was down to just a handful of us, Samantha's side not-so-graciously consented to choose me. They seemed about as excited as if they'd won a free trip to their doctor's office. Finally, dead last, we got Carnie. Jaw clenched, she shuffled over next to me.

"Oh, look. The tacky twosome," Liv commented, loudly enough for everyone to hear. I wanted to give her something tacky right in the face. I shot her my nastiest look, but suddenly Anteles was blasting her whistle again, and the ball was in motion and coming right at me. I dodged.

A few throws later, Jane recovered the ball and launched it full force at Carnie. I watched the ball shoot across the room. Carnie was watching it, too — expressionless, uninterested. She didn't move a muscle. It slammed her right in the thigh.

She flinched, but barely. Without showing any emotion, she moved out of bounds and sat down with her back against the wall of the gym.

"F for ef-fort!" Ms. Anteles yelled.

I swallowed hard. I'd seen Carnie move like lightning when it mattered to that little boy. And who could blame her for opting out of our little war with the dodgeball?

I tried to get her attention. "Are you okay?" I mouthed over to her.

"Brittany!" she yelled back, making frantic motions at some vague spot behind me. I whirled around to see the dodgeball flying straight at me. I ducked. Just in time for the ball to make solid contact with my face.

"Owww!" I screamed. I fell backward, bringing my hands up to my throbbing nose. They came away bloody. SCREE! The whistle blew. Carnie came running over to my side.

"Oh, my god, your nose!" she said. "Is it broken?"

I touched my nose and gingerly wobbled it back and forth. It hurt, but I didn't think I'd broken it. "I don't think so," I said weakly.

Anteles's whistle sounded again. "Williams! Penalty! Face throw. You're outta the game."

Williams!!? I sat up abruptly, and felt the blood rush to my nose again. As in Lisa Williams!? I searched for her across the room and spotted her staring at me in horror.

Lisa had thrown that? The metallic taste of blood flowed into my mouth, but that was the least of it. She came over to where I lay. "Brit, I didn't mean to hurt you," she said, her voice wobbling. "Ms. Anteles — it wasn't on purpose. I mean . . . it would have been below the shoulders if she hadn't ducked right into the path of the ball. . . ."

It would have been below the shoulders!? So Lisa *had* meant to hurl that thing at me. She *had* meant to hurt me. And I *did* hurt. A lot. Not just physically, either. "Save it," I snapped at her.

I refused to sit anywhere near her on the sidelines. I chose a spot with plenty of air between us and concentrated just a little too hard on pressing a tissue against my nose. I wouldn't even look at her. Carnie sat next to me, and we watched the dodgeball fly back and forth.

Oh — by the way, our team won. Big whoop. In the larger picture, I had lost, and I knew it.

Chapter 7

I slammed my locker as hard as I could. It made a crash like a brittle cymbal. But honestly, it didn't make me feel one iota better. My nose was throbbing — I still had a sorry piece of tissue pressed up against it. And the rest of me felt even worse. "I'd rather be a tacky twosome than a phony foursome," I muttered.

Carnie put a hand on my arm. "Brittany, you can't let them get to you, okay?"

I slung my knapsack onto one shoulder. "I know, and I wish that it didn't bother me."

Carnie took a deep breath. "Look, it's not like I wouldn't change things if I could. It's not like I wouldn't like to walk in here one day and have a bunch of people say good morning to me. Or pick me for their team without being scared into it by some ex-Navy Seal, you know? But what kills me? It's not Liv and her Bradford Barbie dolls, okay?" Carnie paused, as if considering what to say next.

"It's that I don't have a single other person at school to share anything with. I mean, until today. Until you. Can I say something, Brittany, and don't take it the wrong way. You and Lisa? I don't exactly know what's going on, but I always basically envied you guys. I mean, I sort of imagined that if I had a best friend, it would be like it is with you guys."

Like me and Lisa? Like having someone write horrible things about you in her diary and assaulting you with deadly dodgeballs? "You're kidding," I said. "I mean, I didn't even realize you noticed us."

"I have a lot of time to myself to observe things," Carnie pointed out. "And to me? Not that my opinion counts so much, but you guys are the cool ones in this school. You seem like you know what's real and what's not. You say what's on your mind. . . ."

"I don't know," I said slowly. "We used to."

"When we were sitting out the rest of the dodgeball game?" Carnie said. "Well, you were so busy not looking at her, you didn't see how upset she was."

"She was upset? I was the one sitting there with a bloody nose!" I waved my tissue around to illustrate.

Carnie pressed her lips together. She was quiet for a moment. "I think you should at least talk to her."

I shut my eyes. If only I could shut out all the anger and hurt that had built up throughout the day like steam in a pressure cooker. Talk to Lisa? Why bother? It was clear from her diary, as well as that wayward dodgeball, that Lisa wasn't interested in being my friend anymore.

"I'll just be a sec," I told Carnie as I headed into the girls' room. My nose had stopped bleeding, and I needed to wash my face.

She nodded. "I'll meet you back at your locker."

But the second my platform sneakers hit the bathroom tiles, I wanted to do a 180 and run. There were Liv and Carole, brushing their hair at the mirror. And Natalia and Jane, sitting up on the window ledge, hanging. They stared as I came in.

"Oooh, everyone, we better get out," Jane said. "We don't want to be contaminated by Carnage's new appendage, Spittany."

I went over to the sink, doing my best to ignore them.

"Oh, but Jane, we don't want to miss the very rare opportunity to watch a major stink bomb actually wash up," Liv said. "What's the occasion? Is Carnage taking you home to her sty to meet the rest of the pigs?"

51

"Carnie," I said. "Her name is Carnie."

"Carnie, Carnage. Smells the same to me," Liv said.

"You know, Spittany," Carole put in, "you set the school speed record today. From random person to incredible loser in one day."

"Why can't you just leave me alone?" I snapped.

Carole raised a perfectly shaped, strawberry-blond eyebrow. "Who, me? I was just brushing my hair."

"That's right," Jane jumped in. "Some people think good grooming is important. Of course, others may disagree." She made a horrid snorting sound and pressed her nose up, pig-style, with her finger.

"The only pigs in here are you!" I retorted. My voice trembled. I felt hot tears spring to my eyes.

"Oooh, Spittany's mad at us," Natalia said. "Spittany doesn't like us. Boo-hoo-hoo." She let loose a mean laugh.

All of a sudden, one of the stall doors opened. "Why don't you and your coven go throw another eye of newt in your cauldron," said a familiar voice. A split second later, Lisa emerged.

Whoa! I blinked hard. It looked like Lisa. It sounded like Lisa. But it was totally un-Lisa-like to spring forward with her claws out like that. I knew it took every bit of guts and courage. She must have been sitting in there, all finished with her reign on the porcelain throne, just trying to work up the nerve to say what she really felt. And suddenly, I just didn't care what Natalia or Liv or any of them said. I smiled at Lisa. She smiled back.

"Well, looks like the pig family's bigger than we thought," Liv harrumphed.

"Yeah, the tacky twosome is really a B.O. trio," Jane said. "Come on, girls. The odor in here is just way too strong for me."

"Bye," I said sticky-sweetly. "Don't cast too many evil spells. Oh, wait, don't forget your broomsticks. . . ." I called after them.

I turned back to Lisa. "Thanks for rescuing me," I said.

"No problem. I mean, it was kind of fun. How's your nose?" she asked.

"Okay. A little bruised, but it's stopped bleeding."

Lisa nodded. We just stood there for a moment. "Listen . . ." we both began in unison. "No, go ahead . . ." we chorused more or less at the same time. We both laughed tentatively.

"Brit — I never meant to hurt you," Lisa said. "I

don't know what got into me when I threw that dodgeball. . . . I guess . . . I was really hurting, too. And angry. And, well, you know how I just hold my anger in sometimes? This time I couldn't hold it and I just sort of exploded. . . . I mean, having you dump me . . . It made me feel so rotten."

"Wait a second," I said. "*I* dumped *you*?"

Lisa looked startled. "Well, Brittany, what else would you call it when you don't show up to hand out flyers with me because you're too busy hanging out with Carnie Bryson? What else do you call it when I keep waiting for you to show up at lunch so we can make up, and you and Carnie cut out and go have some field trip at the mall?" Lisa's voice rose in the echoey bathroom.

I felt my temper flaming up again, too. "You were waiting for me? Gee, it looked like you and Sarah were pretty cozy without me. Was she giving you any good advice on going to slumber parties without certain people who rhyme with witch?"

Lisa groaned. "Brittany, didn't anyone ever tell you that a person's diary is their private, personal property? How much of it did you read, anyway?"

I frowned. "I don't know. Wasn't what I read enough? And before you start wigging out on Carnie, she's not the person you think she is."

Lisa gave a little frown. "Then who is she, Brit? I mean, you never cut school before you started hanging out with her. You never got in trouble with the Torpedo before. And Carnie — well, it's not her first time . . ."

I took a long breath. I wasn't going to get mad at Lisa all over again. I knew it looked one way, even though it was really another. I started at the beginning. "Lis, the bus accident this morning? Well, I was late because I was there." I filled her in on the whole thing. "The mystery hero girl?"

"You mean the one who saved the little boy?"

I nodded. "The rumor mill got that part of the story, but no one would believe who it really was."

"Carnie?" Lisa's big brown eyes widened. "Why . . . didn't she say anything?"

"I guess she gets more attention than she'd like," I said. "And it's not the kind anyone wants. Believe me, I know," I added. I told Lisa everything I'd found out about Carnie on the way to school — about her mother and the baby, and how they struggled. How the stories about Carnie just weren't true. How she'd even come to my rescue, at the cost of detention.

Lisa sighed. "I've never been particularly nice to her."

"You've never been mean to her."

"Maybe not. Still. I don't know . . . maybe the three of us could hang out," Lisa suggested.

"I bet Carnie'd like that."

"Look, I'm really sorry I didn't give you a chance to explain about this morning," Lisa said. "I'm really sorry about . . . well, everything."

"Me too," I said. "Especially about reading your diary."

Lisa started laughing. I wasn't sure what was so funny. She reached into her Guatemalan bag and pulled out the swirly-covered book. "Listen, Brittany, I'm still mad. Really mad. I mean, it was a total invasion of privacy to read my diary. But . . . well, if you were gonna read it, you should have read on a little further. . . ." She opened it to the last page. She was still laughing and shaking her head as she handed it to me.

I wanted in on the joke. I started reading where I'd left off.

Sarah and I were talking about her and Sarah was trying to help me decide what to do about the slumber party invitation I got. Brittany wasn't invited. But even if Brittany and I don't agree on stuff all the time, she's still my best friend. Forever. And who wants to go to some stupid party if your best friend's not going to be there?

I shut the diary. I felt like the biggest jerk. For snooping in Lisa's diary. For not snooping enough. For not having enough faith in our friendship. But if I was a jerk, I was a way lucky jerk. "Same," I said, not quite trusting myself not to get all sappy and teary-eyed. "You're my best friend — forever." I gave Lisa a big best-friend hug.

"Brittany? I really missed you today," Lisa said.

"Me too," I replied. "But you know what, Lis? Today's not over."

The air was sweet from all the rain, and the ground was damp. But the sun had burst through the clouds, casting a glow on the first red and orange leaves of fall.

Lisa and Carnie and I turned down Chestnut Street. "Hey, isn't that the new guy?" Lisa said in a whisper.

My pulse picked up a little. I admit it. And I also admit that I recognized him instantly, even from the back. He seemed to sense that he had company behind him. He turned around.

"Oh, hi!" He smiled his lopsided little smile, with a dimple and everything. If he thought we were the school rejects, he didn't let on.

"Um, hi!" I said. Lisa and Carnie said hello, too.

"Nice day for a walk," he said. "Especially after all the excitement getting to school this morning."

"You were on the bus, weren't you?" I asked.

"Yeah. One of the 'survivors.'" He gave an easy laugh. And up close I could see the little flecks of gold in his eyes. Major crushing happening. "I figured I wouldn't push my luck on the way home. I'm Jack," he said. "Jack Berman. And you're in my Spanish class," he said to me.

I nodded. He'd noticed! Jack Berman had noticed.

"Tiffany, right?" he said.

I felt myself blush. "Brittany," I said. I tried not to be too disappointed, but I got that elevator-going-down feeling.

"Oops. My bad. I'm sorry, Brittany."

"And this is Lisa Williams and Carnie Bryson," I said.

"Hi, Lisa. Hi, Carnie." His gaze lingered on Carnie. His expression grew serious. He'd heard the stories. Elevator going way, way down.

"You know," he said, "the real survivor this morning was that little boy. Maybe certain people don't know it, but you were the most important person there this morning." Elevator going back up.

"How'd you know?" Carnie asked softly.

"I saw what happened out my window," Jack said. "You were there, too, weren't you?" he asked me. "I'm not that great with names, but I never forget a face." So that's why Jack had been staring at us in the Torpedo's office this morning. "Well, it's nice to know all of you," he said. "Really nice."

"Same," we all said, more or less as a trio. "And welcome to Bradford," I added.

"Thanks, Brittany," Jack replied. I smiled to myself, glad he'd gotten my name right the second time around. "I think I'm gonna like it here." He looked right at me as he said that. He really did.

I felt a surge of happiness. Of course Jack was going to like it here. I linked arms with Lisa on one side and Carnie on the other. There were no better people anywhere in the whole world.

What If?

I Almost Missed the Bus ...

by Jennifer Rabin

SCHOLASTIC INC.

New York   Toronto   London   Auckland   Sydney
Mexico City   New Delhi   Hong Kong

ISBN 0-439-08718-X

12 11 10 9 8 7 6 5 4 3 2 1   9/9 0 1 2 3 4/0

Printed in the U.S.A.   40

First Scholastic printing, June 1999

Chapter 1

Some people wake up with plenty of time to get ready for their day. My best friend, Lisa Williams, for example. She sets her alarm so she can lie in bed and wake up slowly — half in and half out of some dreamy cloudland — not that Lisa doesn't tend to visit cloudland even when she's not just waking up, but that's another story. So she has time for a nice, warm shower — Lisa's into all kinds of herbal soaps and aromatherapy shampoos — to start her day balanced and happy.

Me, I guess I'm just not one of those good-morning-sunshine-type people. I hate waking up — maybe because I usually stay up too late listening to my album-du-jour, or working on my Web page, or doing some industrial-strength chatting on-line with the girls in my Web ring. Even when I do the early-to-bed thing, I can't get into the early-to-rise part.

That's why I've got my morning down to a science. The Brittany Elliot don't-miss-a-minute-

1

more-of-sleep-than-you-need-to science. 7:15: Alarm goes off. 7:16: Outta bed. 7:17–7:19: Make bed.

I'll spare you the nitty-gritty details. Suffice it to say that by 7:53, I've done it all, and I'm walking out of the house with exactly enough time to catch the school bus two blocks away, at 7:58. So I'm not the first in line. So what? I make the bus.

Except that on this particular morning, my rhythm was off by a few minutes. 7:52: I slid my feet into my new red platform sneakers and tied them. 7:53: I pulled on my sweater. 7:53 and 30 seconds: I grabbed my loose-leaf binder off my desk and shoved it into my knapsack.

And that's when I really hit a snag. See, one of the books in my bag wasn't mine, and I noticed it instantly. The cover was made out of this swirly lavender-pink-and-sunset-orange paper. Really beautiful handmade paper. The book was Lisa's diary, and she carried it almost everywhere.

Of course I'd seen it a zillion times, but I'd never read it. I mean, Lisa's my best friend. She's been my best friend for practically ever. But a diary's a diary. Besides, Lisa and I don't have any secrets. At least I didn't think we did. . . .

I eased the purple-and-pink-and-orange book

out of my knapsack and stared at it. Well, Lisa *had* been going kind of weird on me lately. Getting all quiet at things I said. Not returning my phone calls. I'd finally said something to her over milk and mint sandwich cookies in my kitchen yesterday, and major spillage had ensued. By that I don't mean we knocked over our milk.

Like she said *I* was going weird on *her.* Making all kinds of comments. Excuse me? I always make comments. Lisa likes my comments. They make her laugh. Or used to.

Now, well . . . I wasn't sure exactly what was going on lately. I ran my finger over the soft, coarse, clothlike paper covering her diary. Maybe the answer was in here.

No. Uh-uh. *Back off, Brittany,* I told myself. I have a diary, too. A plain, basic black diary, like a closed door, and I'd kill anyone who read it. And anyway, I knew what would be in Lisa's diary. At least on the most recent page. Lisa would have written all about "the big talk" in my kitchen. And I already knew about that. Every word of it.

See, while I thought Lisa was giving me the old brush-off, she thought I was giving it to her. She said I made fun of all the stuff she was serious

3

about, and why should she call me back when I wouldn't want to do any of the things she wanted to do, anyway. Like Operation Clean Harbor.

Then it started making a little more sense. Lisa had been bugging me, in her own quiet way, to pass out leaflets at school before homeroom about the pipeline they wanted to build in Bradford Harbor and all the incredibly gross sewage that would spew into the water. I'd been complaining and basically trying to get out of it.

I mean, I'm all for a clean Bradford Harbor. Totally. And I applaud Lisa's concern. It's part of the reason she's my best bud. She knows what's important. She should be voted as eighth grader most likely to save the planet. But Lisa kind of knows it too much sometimes. Like if she had her way, we'd be spending all — and I mean all — our free time saving the whales and feeding the world — and Lisa would bake all the bread to do it by herself. She's the most generous person in the world and I love her for it, but sometimes she's just not the most practical.

"Lis, you really think passing out some leaflets is gonna do anything?" I asked, scarfing a cookie.

Her round face, framed by red hair, crinkled up. "Are you saying I'm wasting my time?" she asked.

"I'm saying people like Liv and Carole and them

4

are just going to throw those leaflets away." Liv and Carole were two of the "we're all that" girls at school. "They'd only care if the pipeline was going to spew into Banana Republic or Nine West."

For once, Lisa didn't laugh at my sharp-edged observation. "Not everyone's like them, Brittany. Some people care about our planet and the world we live in. But apparently you're not one of them."

"Aw, come on, Lis. It's not that I don't care. You know that. But I mean, handing out a bunch of paper . . . If you really want to do something, go down to the harbor and lie down on the beach so they can't get the bulldozers or the pieces of pipeline onto the sand."

I am just more confrontational than Lisa. More up-front. That, and I usually used the time before homeroom to catch up on the homework I hadn't finished the night before.

Lisa arched an eyebrow. "Good idea. But people have to know what's going on before they'll do that."

We kept talking like that for a while. And even though it was about the harbor, it was really about me and Lisa, too. Who respected whom. Who invited whom. Who called. Who cared. The "who's a more loyal friend" show.

In the end, we kind of made up and I agreed to

meet Lisa before homeroom and give out some leaflets. 'Cause it meant so much to her, and she's my best friend.

So things hadn't been so smooth between us lately, and here I was in possession of her diary. A person could be excused for thinking it was fate that the diary ended up in my room right when Lisa had been acting so weird with me. Of course, I don't believe in fate. That's more Lisa's deal.

Totally honestly? Totally, totally? It could have gone either way. I mean, what if I read it? Lisa wouldn't be any the wiser. What you don't know can't hurt you. And besides, I was dying of curiosity.

"Brittany! Hurry up!" That was my sister Charlee calling from downstairs. Charlee's taking a year off between high school and college, and working as a teaching assistant. Getting life experience, she calls it. "You'll miss the bus! I'm leaving for work in two seconds, and I'm already late, so I can't drive you!"

I took a deep breath, flipped open Lisa's diary . . . and slammed it shut as soon as I got the barest glimpse of her familiar round handwriting. I couldn't do it. I wouldn't. I shoved the diary back into my knapsack and glanced at the clock. 7:55 and change. More than two minutes off. My pulse shot up. I was outta there.

Chapter 2

Platform sneakers. The sneakers part sounds like you could really run in them. Like to catch a bus, just for example. The platform part — well . . . they look good. Really good. But racing to where the school bus stopped was like trying to do a sprint with blocks strapped to the bottoms of my feet. I had to do this flat-footed kind of trot and be careful not to turn my ankle.

Meanwhile, it was pouring — one of those cold October rains we get in New England — and I didn't have a second to go back for an umbrella. I kept running — trotting, whatever — my face wet, the rain dripping off the ends of my black hair. As I turned the corner, still a block away, I could easily see the bright yellow school bus, its doors open as it picked up passengers. Most of the kids who got on at my stop had boarded already, and as I went from trot to awkward canter, I could see the last person getting on.

"Wait! Wait!" I waved my arms and yelled. I turned on the speed for the burst to the finish line. I was almost there. I saw the bus doors closing. "No!" The bus was pulling away. I took several more strides. I saw the bus stop again. The doors opened. The driver had spotted me.

Thank goodness! I clomped up the bus stairs, wet and breathing hard. A person who believed in fate could be excused for thinking this was my reward for not reading Lisa's diary. If I'd read even two words of it, I definitely would have missed the bus. "Thank you," I panted to Mrs. Jackson, the driver.

"You're welcome, baby," she said. Mrs. Jackson was a large woman with coffee-and-cream skin, a blue uniform, and a perfect record for getting her kids to school safely and on time. She called everyone on her route "baby," but she didn't take any nonsense. "Now go get yourself a seat and buckle up, quick like a bunny. It's slow enough on a rainy day as it is." She waited for me to get seated before she pulled away again.

I made my way down the aisle, looking for an empty seat. Lisa's on a different bus route, so I usually sit next to Sarah G. Sarah moved into my neighborhood last year, and she's pretty nice. Not

to be confused with Sarah P., a friend of mine and Lisa's who we've known since elementary school. Anyway, Sarah — G., that is — was already sitting with Ellen Pines. "Hi," they said as I went by, dripping. "You almost didn't make it," Ellen added. Like, duh, Ellen. Thanks for the news flash.

Liv Magnuson sat behind them with Natalia Lopez. Natalia wasn't quite as all that as Liv's two other ladies-in-waiting, Carole and Jane, but she was the closest thing to it on this bus route, so she and Liv sat together every day. We all kind of smiled this fake hello, but I knew Liv and Natalia were taking in my drowned rat look and feeling superior because they'd remembered their umbrellas, to protect their shiny, perfectly blow-dried hair.

I glanced around, but all the other seats in the front half of the bus were taken. And most of the back half, too. Something about a rainy day. I guess the bus was packed with all the bike-to-school crowd, who left the wheels in the garage.

Stephanie Smith, my second seating choice, was wedged into a window seat next to Robbie Cavaluzzi, who was chowing down on some kind of swollen sandwich. I could smell the spicy tomato sauce as I got up to them. Robbie always had some odoriferous leftover for breakfast on the run. Or

9

roll, to be more precise. Stephanie shook her head at me. I flashed her a sympathetic look and headed farther back. Even Bethany Roberts, this seventh grader who kind of thinks I'm cool and who's kind of my last choice to sit with, had already given up the seat next to her to some other girl in her grade.

No biggie. It's just a bus ride, and not even a very long one. I spotted one empty seat in the way back. And in the same glance, I spotted the random stranger sitting next to the one empty seat. Correction. Not a random stranger, but a *really cute* random stranger. This guy I'd never seen before — because believe me, I would have remembered — with wavy, sandy-colored hair and a smattering of freckles across the bridge of his nose, with full lips and deep-set eyes, and . . . well, let's just say the sum of his parts added up to serious crush material.

I headed toward the empty seat. I mean, it was the only one — so where else was I supposed to head?

Even though I don't believe in fate, I just might start believing a little. I mean, if I'd been on time, maybe I would have been one of the first kids on the bus at my stop, and maybe there would have still

been a free seat or two up front, and maybe I wouldn't have walked all the way back and found myself buckling up next to this total babe magnet. And maybe this really was my reward for not reading the diary.

Of course, as soon as I got over my initial stupor at how I'd lucked out, I remembered that my hair was dripping and my clothes were wet and droopy. Maybe I wasn't as lucky as I thought.

But the hottie smiled this really cute smile — a lopsided smile, with a dimple and everything. "Shower's free. Too bad they don't give you a towel around this resort."

I laughed. "I forgot my umbrella," I said. And then I hated myself. How lame a comment was that? So much for a witty first impression.

He shrugged. "I don't use one. I mean, I used to, but I'd always lose it or leave it somewhere, so I decided, what's the point? It rains. You get wet. You get dry."

On second look, I noticed that *his* hair was wet, too. And that his eyes were gray with flecks of gold in them. "I guess that's one way of looking at it," I said. "Um, I'm Brittany Elliot."

"Jack. Berman."

Jack Berman. I repeated his name to myself

silently. Jack Berman, and he seemed as nice as he was cute. "I, um, haven't seen you around before," I said.

"Yeah, we just moved here," he said. "Today's my first day. Eighth grade," he added.

Yes!! "Me too!" I said. "I mean eighth. Not my first day. Hardly. I mean, I've never gone to school anywhere but good ole Bradford."

Jack kind of sighed. "Can't imagine that. I went to first and second grade in California, third and fourth in New Mexico, and fifth through part of eighth in Ohio."

"Really? Wow, that's kind of cool. I mean, the farthest west I've ever been is to visit my cousins in Pennsylvania."

"Yeah, well, I guess it keeps things interesting," Jack said.

I laughed. Cute, nice, *and* funny. And amazingly easy to talk to. I mean, how often is it that you sit down next to a babe magnet and find yourself anything but tongue-tied? No doubt by this afternoon, all the eighth-grade girls were going to be swarming all over the guy like bees to honey. But here I was, talking to him.

I asked him what had brought him to our fair town of Bradford — well, not so fair today, with the

rain pounding against the bus window in sheets. Though actually it felt pretty cozy to be bump, bump, bumping along in the back of the bus, listening to Jack explain that his parents' jobs kept them on the move a lot. His dad was a journalist and his mom was an illustrator. Kind of more glamorous than my father the dentist and my mother the part-time bookkeeper. Still, Jack seemed to think it might be okay to do the "stable family, pillar of the community, know everyone in school" thing at some point. That scene was way familiar. It reminded me of that expression: One man's ceiling is another man's floor.

"So do you have, like, first-day jitters?" I asked as the bus made one last stop on Caroline Street and a sixth grader got on. I still got them after summer vacation, even though it was mostly the same people from the year before. But Jack looked pretty calm.

"I've got enough experience being the new kid," he said. "You know, been there, done that, bought the T-shirt." We both laughed. "But . . . well, I guess to be perfectly honest, I'm a little bit . . . apprehensive. You know, where's the library, which teacher lets you slide on homework, where will I sit in the cafeteria. Oh, this spot's reserved for the

jocks and other kings? Well, excuse me. Shoot, you mean I picked the table with the total losers?"

Now I was really laughing hard. The guy got it. His ceiling might be my floor, but I felt like we looked at things in a similar way. "The table closest to the kitchen? Losers," I informed him. "The one near the back door? Jocks. Except when the weather's nice they usually take their trays outside and sit in the bleachers at the field. Them and the 'all that' girls."

"All that and a bag of fat-free, baked-not-fried, please-I'm-on-a-diet chips?" Jack cracked.

"You got it," I said.

"Well, see?" Jack said. "Those are the things you have to figure out fast when you're the new kid."

Suddenly, I heard myself offering to show him around. Help him learn the ropes. A bold move, but it just felt so easy to be with him.

His dimpled smile told me it had been the right move. "That'd be cool," he said. "Thanks, Tiffany."

My own smile slipped a little. Here I was deciding the guy was my new best friend — well, second best after Lisa — and he didn't even know my name. "Brittany," I said.

He looked embarrassed. "Brittany. I'm sorry. I'm not good with —"

HONK! SCREEEECH!! The blare of the bus horn and a metallic squeal of wet brakes pierced the air. My breath stuck in my throat as the bus fishtailed wildly. I heard the angry honk of another car horn outside. The next couple of seconds seemed to go in slow motion, as if I were experiencing time through the wide end of a telescope. Out the window, I saw we were veering off the road, away from a little boy in a yellow rain slicker, who was being yanked out of the street by a girl in a shapeless beige raincoat. Wait. That looked like . . . Carnie Bryson. Carnage, we called her behind her back. But I didn't have time to give Carnage a second thought before we skidded away from her and the little boy, and the road and trees were a blur and I was vaguely aware of my own scream mingling with the screams of everyone else on the bus and we were sliding, sliding, sliding. . . .

Chapter 3

BOOM! I jolted forward against my seat belt, to the sick sound of shattering glass and crumpling metal. And then it was quiet. A full moment of absolute, dead silence. It was during this moment that I moved my head around and bent my arms and patted my legs and assured myself I was in one piece. I glanced over at Jack. He looked frightened but fine. So did everyone else around me.

Then someone up in the front of the bus began to cry softly, but it sounded more like relief than fear. I unbuckled my seat belt and stood up. I could see that the front of the bus, near the doors, had hit a tree. The bus was crushed around it, the windshield missing a jagged piece of glass. The stairs and front landing were smashed like a broken accordion. We weren't getting off this bus the way we'd gotten on. Knapsacks and lunch boxes littered the aisles.

But nobody was badly hurt. That was the main

thing. Almost as soon as we stopped, Mrs. Jackson was up and checking on her babies. She wanted everyone to stay in the bus because of the rain. When the ambulance and the police arrived, we'd have to jump out the emergency exit. James Laufer, who'd been in my fifth-grade class, hadn't bothered to put on his seat belt, and he had a bump on his head that was growing bigger and more colorful by the second, but he said he could still recite all the states in alphabetical order, so he must be okay. The sixth grader who'd gotten on at the last stop had hurt his arm. A few kids up by the doors had some bruises and scratches, and poor Stephanie was wearing Robbie's sandwich on her shirt. We were darned lucky that was the worst of it, and we knew it.

"Welcome to Bradford," I said to Jack, after we'd established that everyone was all right. My voice was still shaky.

"I guess I can honestly say my first day's started out as a crashing success," he managed to joke back.

So there we were — stuck on the bus until the police cars and the fire trucks and the EMS vans rolled up with their sirens blaring, to set us free. I couldn't help but be impressed at how helpful Jack

was — matching people up with their bags and personal belongings, comforting the sixth grader whose arm had gotten hurt.

"So you know the one about the patient with the broken arm?" he asked gently. "The doctor's putting the final wrapping on the cast, and he tells the patient he'll be good as new in a couple of months. The patient asks, 'Doc, will I be able to play the violin?' And the doctor tells him, 'Sure.' The patient gets this big, goofy grin on his face and he says, 'Gee, Doc, that's great, 'cause I couldn't play the violin before!'"

Everyone on the bus kind of groaned and giggled. The sixth grader did, too, and it seemed to make him less frightened about his arm.

Suddenly, Liv Magnuson was easing her willowy, auburn-haired self down next to the sixth grader. "You know, I broke my arm in the fourth grade," she said to him, but she was looking straight at Jack. "I tried to jump my horse, Wonder, but I fell. Anyway, my arm healed fine. No big deal." She flashed a toothpaste smile while she talked, and made her big brown eyes even bigger.

Okay, so the cat was out of the bag about the cute new boy. Liv had discovered him. And she intended for him to discover her. Not that I could

really blame her. But didn't she get enough attention as it was?

Jack looked at her and smiled. My stomach did one of those elevator-going-down-too-fast deals. But then he looked back at the sixth grader. "You'll be okay," he assured him. "Besides, if it's broken, a cast looks way cool. I'll sign it. So will Brittany." He didn't have any trouble with my name the second time. Elevator going back up.

"We all will," Liv said, and this time she included me in the bright shower of her smile. Totally honestly? Totally, totally? On the one hand, I thought, *What a fake,* and I wanted her to stay away from Jack. But on the other hand, I felt kind of special being part of Liv's little world. And even more special being part of Jack's.

Eventually the whole caravan of cars and trucks and uniformed officials arrived, and I have to say it was pretty exciting, with all those lights flashing and sirens screaming. They lifted us out through the emergency windows one by one, sheltered us under roomy umbrellas, checked our vital signs, and made doubly sure we were all okay.

My pulse was beating too fast, but they didn't need to know it was the effect of a certain lopsided smile and not the crash. Okay, maybe a little of

both. Then they asked us all some questions about what had happened, and it was only at that point that I remembered Carnie.

Carnie — Carnage — Bryson was the girl you didn't want to get stuck with for a science partner. The girl you didn't want to sit near in class. The girl you crossed the street to avoid. Okay, I'm not really proud to say that, but it's true.

Carnage always looked like a total wreck. Her clothes were ancient. And I don't mean vintage. Hey, I've gotten some of my fave outfits at Secondhand Rose. Like my beaded sweater and my faded, wide-bell jeans. But I'm getting off the subject. See? I don't even like to *talk* about Carnage Bryson. But the point is, she dressed in seriously used. Threadbare, stained. People said she smelled bad, too — a fact I hadn't gotten close enough to confirm, thank you. Carnage was always getting to school late and I heard she cut classes and that her brother might be in jail. Whatever. The girl was scary. I looked around for her. The little kid in the rain slicker was being interviewed by a policewoman, but Carnage was nowhere to be seen. What had she been doing, anyway? Had she pushed the little kid out into the street?

But the word got around fast — as it always

does. The little kid was crossing the street. Suddenly, he'd seen the bus coming straight at him, and he'd frozen. Some girl — the little boy didn't know her name — had come up from behind him and yanked him out of harm's way. She'd stayed with him until the police arrived, telling him jokes and making sure he wasn't scared. But as soon as help arrived, she'd taken off. She was quickly christened the mystery hero.

I felt instantly bad for thinking Carnage had pushed the little boy. I mean Carnie. I was fairly sure that's who it had been, outside my bus window. But Carnie, a hero? It didn't fit in with everything else I'd heard. And if she was a hero, why hadn't she stuck around to bathe in a little glory?

We got to miss half the morning at school. Which meant that I got to spend half the morning with Jack. If I wasn't rocking a major crush the moment I saw him, I definitely was by the time we got to school on the backup bus they'd sent to the crash site. We discovered we were both die-hard fans of Junk Sail — especially their latest album. We traded homepage addresses. In addition, Jack had been totally amazing. He was just genuinely nice.

But when we stepped through the doors to

school, he got a little shy. We just happened to show up between second and third periods, right when everyone was changing classes. As soon as the word went out, everyone came running to rally around the survivors. That's what we were now. The survivors. Like we'd just made it through a tidal wave on the high seas or something. Well, everyone likes a little drama in their day. Especially if it means you get to miss the first ten minutes of your next class. In any event, the story of the accident had somehow preceded us. We were famous. At least for today.

Jack stuck close to my side, at the center of all the attention. It had to be overwhelming. Even for a guy who'd bought the new kid T-shirt in every color.

I saw Lisa edging through the crowd and hurrying over. "Brittany!" she cried. She threw her arms around me. "Oh, my god, I'm so glad you're safe! I was so worried when I heard."

I hugged her back. "We're all okay. It could have been a lot worse. I mean a whole lot."

"Well, I'm just so, so relieved it wasn't," she said. "Totally, totally." I suddenly felt all warm and fuzzy. I really did. I mean, Lisa is a true friend. Even if she *was* acting a little weird lately. That happened with friends. Right? I eased out of the hug and gave Lisa

a smile. She smiled back. Then she kind of glanced over at Jack and back at me.

"Oh, hey, Lis, this is Jack. Berman. He just moved to Bradford. Jack, this is Lisa. My best friend," I added.

"Nice to meet you," Jack said, and flashed Lisa the lopsided, dimpled smile.

Meanwhile, I spied Liv a few feet away from us, surrounded by her court. Natalia was still with her, and Carole Johannsen and Jane Bonner had joined them. Carole had added the *e* to the end of her name at the beginning of junior high. Like that dumb *e* made her more glamorous or something. But Jane didn't need a fancy name to be glamorous. With her delicate features, long, straight flaxen-blond hair, and up-to-the-second clothes that she and her mother got on frequent shopping trips to Boston's trendiest boutiques, she was plenty glamorous all on her own.

The guys thought so, too. Half the junior high football team was in love with Jane. Sometimes I thought Liv was friends with her just so she wouldn't have her as a rival. Of course, Liv had her share of admirers of the male persuasion, too. They flocked around her now — the jocks and kings, as Jack had called them. But Liv wasn't paying much

attention to them. Instead, she looked over at us — at Jack, actually — and waved. "That guy was awesome," she told her friends, purposely loud enough for us to hear. "He was so great with the younger kids, and he kept the rest of us in stitches." She flashed us her pearly whites again.

Jack gave this little wave back. I did, too. Lisa looked at me and frowned. She didn't say anything, but her expression did. Waving at one of *them*? she was thinking. We'd always reserved our deepest scorn for those girls. All that brand-new, expensive clothing. All that smugness. All that attitude that said, *We're better than you*. But I mean, what was I supposed to do when Liv waved?

"So . . . I was thinking maybe we could hand out the Clean Harbor leaflets at lunch," Lisa finally said. "Since we didn't get to do it this morning."

Right. In all the excitement this morning, I'd forgotten about the pamphlets. I felt a tiny little jolt of annoyance. Jeez, I'd almost met the Big Cheese, bit the big one, bought the family farm — pick your own silliest expression for *died* — and Lisa was already rescheduling our good deed of the day. "Can't we give it a tiny rest for today?" I asked.

Mistake. I knew it the second the words were out of my mouth. Most people didn't know it when Lisa

got her righteous and angry on. She didn't scream. She didn't get out of control. But her blue eyes flashed like a knife in the sun. "See?" she said, a coolness in her voice. "I knew you didn't want to do it!"

I sighed. "Look, it's been a crazy morning, okay? I just . . . would kind of like to chill at lunch. We can do the leaflets tomorrow, okay?"

Lisa shrugged. "Okay."

"Good. Well, I guess Jack and I are supposed to go to the Torpedo's office and get late passes," I said. The Torpedo was our principal, Ms. Torpe. "Catch you at lunch?"

Lisa nodded. "Same time, same channel."

"We can tell Jack all about the hierarchy of seating in the cafeteria, right?"

Lisa broke down and gave a little laugh. "The cultural anthropology of Bradford Junior High?" Lisa's parents were both professors, so she said things like that. "That should be interesting."

It was only after she walked away that I remembered I still had her diary in my knapsack.

Chapter 4

We "survivors" got our late passes from the Torpedo's office. She gave Jack his class schedule, too. "I trust the rest of your first day will go more smoothly than it began," she said crisply. Somehow, she managed to make it sound as if it were Jack's fault that he'd started the morning off like this.

Jack shifted a little uncomfortably, from one Doc Marten to the other. I could see him taking in the Torpedo's icy-blond helmet of hair, whipped into submission with an arsenal of sprays and gels, and her wrinkle-free, sensible suit. "Well, Brittany volunteered to show me around, so I'm sure it will," he said tentatively.

We took our passes and beat a hasty retreat out of Torpedo range. "Is she always so . . . welcoming?" Jack whispered.

"The Torpedo's special that way," I whispered back.

At that moment, I noticed Carnie Bryson slip-

ping into the office. I stared at her as she went over to the desk and lined up for a late pass with the remaining "survivors." Sure enough, she wore that same baggy beige raincoat I'd seen out the bus window. She had to have been the one who'd saved the little boy.

Liv, standing near us, was watching her, too. Carnie accepted her pass as if she were one of the "survivors." "Liar," Liv hissed as Carnie turned around.

Carnie stared back. Her face was hard.

"No way she was on the bus. We would have smelled her," Liv said.

Ouch. Should I say something? Come to Carnie's defense? But Carnie just scowled harder. At Liv. And then at me. Her green eyes gleamed with fury. What had I done? Defend Carnage? Forget it. Why should I defend someone who was shooting bullets at me with her eyes? Why should I defend someone who didn't even bother to defend herself? She stormed past us.

"What's up with her?" Jack asked.

"You don't want to know," Liv answered. "Does he, Brittany?"

"You definitely don't, Jack," Natalia answered for me, getting in a word with Jack herself.

I watched Carnie's back disappear out of the office. Was Carnie a liar? A hero? Both?

The Torpedo saved me from thinking about it further. "Boys and girls. If you don't want to miss any more of the morning, I suggest you get moving. Miss Elliot? You say you're going to show Mr. Berman to class? You'd better do it now. You've already missed enough of the day."

We all hupped to. When the Torpedo spoke, you listened.

Everyone should spend one morning escorting a babe magnet around his new school — it's an experience. One by one, the girls shot Jack a gooey look or two. But it was only Liv and her ladies who had the self-confidence, the bravery, the sheer nerve to be totally, ridiculously obvious. Ladies and gentleman, I introduce the following evidence:

Exhibit A: Liv. The second we were out of the Torpedo's office, she and Natalia caught up to Jack and me in the hall. Liv pointed to the schedule in his hand. "Let's see what you pulled," she said. Suddenly, she was practically yanking it away from him. But with a perfect smile, of course.

"Be my guest," Jack said mildly. But his crack was lost on Liv, who was already studying the

schedule as intently as if it were an end-of-the-year exam. Natalia looked over her shoulder at it, too.

"Let's see. Science with Mr. Yallowitz," Liv said. "Our friend Carole's in your class. She says Yallowitz is really funny. Advanced Spanish with Garrido. That's your class, isn't it, Natalia?" It happened to be my class, too, but Liv didn't give either of us time to get a word in edgewise. "Oh, and look, Jack! We're in English together!" Her voice got as smooth and light as a silk nightie. "Maybe we can help each other study!"

Well, she wanted to study something with Jack, that was for sure. But I didn't think English was precisely what she had in mind.

"Maybe," Jack repeated politely.

Exhibit B: Carole. Don't forget the *e*. She got to him in science. When I picked him up after class to walk to Spanish, there she was coming out of the room with him, attached to his side like they were magnets. "So if you need someone to catch you up on our electricity unit, just say," she offered him, giving a toss of her shiny, strawberry-blond hair. Electricity. Right. Like the electricity between a girl and a boy, maybe? "Oh, hi, Brittany," she said as an afterthought.

"Hi, Carole," I answered, surprised — and I

admit, maybe just a little flattered — to find out she knew my name.

Exhibit C: Natalia. She took her turn in Spanish class. And what a turn. First of all, she was out of Liv's shadow. Liv took French — the better to shop in Paris with one day, my dear. Second, Natalia was the best Spanish student in the class. This had a lot to do with the fact that her grandfather was Mexican. She'd been hearing Spanish most of her life, and she spoke it beautifully. Third — and here's the part where she just got lucky — Jack's Spanish turned out to be excellent, too. "They started us early in California," Jack explained to me.

Whatever the reason, Mr. Garrido saw an opportunity. He asked Natalia and Jack to read the dialogue in our textbook together.

Jack, reading the character of Raphael, began. I'll translate, for those of you who don't take Spanish. "'What would you like to do this afternoon?'" Jack/Raphael read.

Well, Natalia, reading the part of Luz, gave Jack this look with her big, dark eyes — I can only call it smoldering. "'I'd like to leave by the first train for Segovia,'" she said, all low and throaty, as if she were asking him out on a private date.

Jack played it cool. I guess Jack was used to this kind of thing. "'Segovia?'" he said. And let me tell you, that's not such an easy place to pronounce. I can't do it without tripping over my tongue. But Jack said it perfectly. "'What a beautiful city!'"

"'Yes, and I know of a wonderful restaurant,'" Natalia/Luz continued, as if they were the only two people in the room. In the world, maybe.

Well, to make a longish story short, by the time they finished reading, you could almost see some grown-up version of Jack and Natalia sharing a romantic, candlelit dinner in a dark little restaurant in the middle of old Spain. It was an awesome performance.

"*Adiós,* Raphael," Natalia said to Jack flirtatiously at the end of class. "*Adiós,* Brittany," she added. "*Hasta luego, amigos.*" Translation: See ya, pals. This was the first time I'd been Natalia Lopez's pal.

Jane, on the other hand, didn't resort to theatrics. She was exhibit D. As in glaringly Direct. We were at the lockers right before lunch, when Jane came up and handed Jack her card. Yup. Jane actually had a business card. A cream-colored card, embossed around the edges with a delicate pink ribbon design. *Jane Bonner*, it read in elegant type.

Under her name was her address. And her phone number.

But just as I was about to look at Jack and roll my eyes, Jane turned the charm on me. "Oh, by the way, Brittany, I *love* those shoes."

Against my better judgment, I felt a tickle of pride. Jane of the fab wardrobe loved my platform sneakers! Maybe it had been worth running after the bus in the rain this morning.

Okay, so I knew that Jane and Liv and them wouldn't have given me the time of day if it weren't for Jack. Still, it felt sort of good to have the most popular girls in school paying so much attention to me. I had to be honest. The way coolest girls in my school were suddenly my pals.

I rest my case.

Chapter 5

Jack and I snaked our way through the lunch line, cracking each other up. "Whoa, amazing! They had this exact same food in my last school," Jack said. "And I mean the exact same. Like this very piece of —"

"— three-month-old mystery meat?" I finished. We pushed our trays along the steel bars. "Come on, it's good for you. All the chewy-chewy-chewing builds strong teeth." I selected a plate of gluey-looking macaroni and cheese — the lesser of several evils.

Jack made the same choice. "You ever think there must be one humongous, central kitchen down underground in the middle of the country? And there are, like, all these delivery shoots leading to every school in every state . . ."

I laughed and helped myself to half an apple, the white part quickly going brown. "Sometimes my mom makes me a bag lunch," I said. "But she was

late getting my little sister to school this morning. I guess it kind of runs in the family. . . ."

Jack filled a paper cup with ginger ale. I grabbed some orange soda, and we carried our trays off the cafeteria line. I glanced around the lunchroom. It was already half filled with kids at rows of identical long tables and benches. In the center of the room, James Laufer and some of the rowdier element were busy flinging Jell-O shots with their spoons. James's swollen eye was impressive under the fluorescent lights. A few kids at quieter tables were trying to study. Emphasis on *trying. Give it up, guys,* I thought. It was too noisy in the big room.

I guess we'd gotten here before Lisa, because she wasn't in our usual spot. My eyes swept the other tables, just in case. Nope. No Lisa. But I did spot Liv. Actually, it was hard to miss her. She was waving her hands over her head to invite us over to her table. The one by the back door, like I'd told Jack. The one with the most popular girls and boys in school.

"Jocks and fat-free chips?" Jack asked lightly.

I was torn. I mean, I'd never been invited over to that table before. And it was, well, a sort of Bradford Junior High honor, you know? Of course,

I'd told Lisa I'd see her at lunch. And they weren't going to invite Lisa over to their table. But Lisa was nowhere to be seen at this second. And Liv and company were waiting for us. To the best of my knowledge, no one had ever refused an audience at Queen Liv's table. "Why not?" I asked, more casually than I felt.

Jack arched one eyebrow. "Whatever," he said.

As we carried our trays to their table, I told myself it was good to be open to new people and new experiences. The day had started out unlike any other, so why shouldn't it continue that way? Besides, I was beginning to see that those girls might have a redeeming quality or two. Like good taste in platform sneakers, for one. And new cute boys, for another.

Confession: It was fun sitting at the Number One table. Even with the rain still coming down outside, I just kind of felt as if there were a special flood of sunlight streaming in through the windows onto this table in the lunchroom. I knew everyone else wished they were sitting where I was sitting. Bill Davies, the starting quarterback, was there, and his friends Tim Pike and Josh DeBeers. Josh had this

sun-kissed, baggy-jeaned, surfer thing going, and I'd been secretly crushing on him all through seventh grade. And though now he seemed so much less . . . worthy than Jack, I still got a little thrill when he said hi to me.

"Oh, hey, you two," Jane said as we sat down. (And boy did I like the way that sounded.) "You absolutely *must* try some of this marvelous cold poached salmon with lemon chiffonade. It's left over from my parents' dinner party." She pushed forward a container of silky pink fish bathed in creamy, pale yellow sauce.

"Chiffonade, huh?" Jack said, and I had a feeling he was making fun of it. But we both had to agree it beat the macaroni and cheese, hands down.

Liv showed off her armful of new Lucite bangles in different rainbow colors, and then she took them off and all the girls took turns trying them on. I felt very much included.

Still, part of me was feeling seriously, severely guilty. Your basic mouse in a cheese shop. When I saw Lisa walk into the lunchroom, this part kicked into overdrive. It wasn't even as if I was keeping an eagle eye out for her. In fact, it would have been easier if I'd managed not to see her. But I just sort of felt it when she pushed through the heavy swing-

ing doors that led into the cafeteria. You know how it is when you're really connected to someone. Well, Lisa and I are really connected. Or at least we used to be.

I mean, how many other thirteen-year-old girls actually agree with me that *Titanic* was a total snore-bore? How many other girls my age couldn't believe how long it took for that ship to go down — like you knew it right from the beginning, but you had to wait about an hour and a half for it to happen. Who else breathed a sigh of relief when the iceberg appeared on the screen and said, "Finally! Well, it's about time." But I'm getting off the subject. That was in better days.

Anyway, Lisa seemed to sense me, too. Her gaze zoomed straight to me. I started to raise my hand in greeting. Slowly. Uncertainly. I wasn't fast enough. Was that on purpose? Was it pure nervousness? You decide. Whatever, I should have been quicker on the draw. By the time my hand was fully up, Lisa had turned away abruptly.

I watched her storm off toward the food line. No, that's not right. Lisa doesn't storm. I'm the type to storm. Lisa walked away stiffly, holding in her anger the way she does.

I tried to get back into the whole sunny, happy,

"we are the world" mode at the table. Jack was talking about being a brown belt in tae kwon do. Like Buffy. And while I thought that was way cool — much cooler than being, say, yet another run-of-the-mill, popular football player, I was distracted by Lisa. I couldn't help sneaking glances as she got her lunch and carried her tray to our unglamorous but perfectly okay usual table.

She sat down next to Sarah P. I could have gone over there. I could have, but I didn't. I took a bite of my mealy apple. A few seconds later, I saw Lisa pull a stack of those leaflets out of the Guatemalan woven shoulder bag she carried her books in. Sarah slid over close to her. I saw Sarah nod. I bit my lip. Sarah was the good friend. Sarah was the one concerned with the harbor and the whales and baking bread for the hungry. I felt a tickle of jealousy. Followed by annoyance. So I was sitting here enjoying myself. Was that some kind of misdemeanor? I was branching out in my friendships.

I must have been staring at Lisa, and Jack must have followed my gaze. "Weren't you supposed to have lunch with her?" he asked softly.

"I, um, she could have come over," I said uncomfortably. But I knew that wasn't true. You didn't eat lunch at this table unless you were invited.

"Oh," Jack said. Was it my imagination, or did he furrow his eyebrows in a tiny, almost imperceptible frown? Then he turned and got into a conversation that the guys were having about basketball.

Why did I feel like my little patch of special sunlight had just been blotted out by a big, gray rain cloud?

Chapter 6

I didn't see Lisa again until English class. I can't remember the last time we didn't stop at our lockers together after lunch. This time I went with Jack, and Lisa wasn't anywhere in sight. And totally honestly? Totally, totally? I didn't seek her out myself, basically because I was feeling pretty weird about everything.

I thought about it all through math. Maybe we were friends out of habit. Maybe we were friends because we'd always been friends. But what kind of friend kept you from making new friends? "One is silver and the other gold." Or so the song says.

I thought about it as I walked through the halls from math to English. Lisa was exceptionally buddy-buddy with Sarah P. So why should I feel so bad about Liv and them?

But the second I saw Lisa sitting there in English class, purposely not looking up as I came into the room, I felt this tugging in my chest. There was my

best friend in the whole world. Her diary was still in my knapsack. I hadn't read it because we kept no secrets from each other. I hadn't read it because I respected her too much. This whole thing was crazy. I went over to her.

"Lis . . ." I waited until she looked up. There was hurt in her blue eyes. I had to swallow against the lump rising in my throat. I was hurting, too. "Lis, they invited me," I whispered.

"Whatever," Lisa said in a small voice. I wished she would just explode and yell at me or something. But then, I usually did the exploding for both of us. "Lisa, I'm sorry. Maybe I was wrong."

She pressed her lips together. Kids filed in around us and took their seats. I know people were looking at us.

"Look, you're my best friend," I said, my voice wavering.

"I am?" She raised a doubtful eyebrow.

God, she could be so stubborn in her own quiet way. If she couldn't keep the harbor clean, no one could. I felt this wave of affection well up in me. "You are," I said. I shrugged off my knapsack, opened it, and reached inside for her diary. "I don't know how I got it," I said. "It was in with my books." I put it on her desk.

Lisa ran her fingers over the lavender-pink-and-orange cover. "Oh, wow! I was going totally nuts trying to find this."

"I didn't read it," I added.

I saw a parade of emotions cross her face — relief, then surprise, then . . . disappointment!? What was up with that? No. I must be reading her wrong.

But Lisa's round face crinkled up. She was quiet for a long, tense moment. "See?" she finally said. "You don't give two shakes about what I'm really thinking, deep down . . ."

Hello!? Anyone home!? I wasn't hearing this. I absolutely could not believe this. I exploded. At least one of us was capable of it. "Excuse me?" I thundered. I knew everyone in the class was tuned in to the Brit and Lisa show, but I was in way too deep to care. "I showed you the consideration, the respect, the . . . *everything* not to read your diary. And you're mad at me for that!!? You really *are* going totally nuts."

"Shh," Lisa said, looking mortified at the unwanted attention. And then Ms. Halvorson was striding over from the front of the room, and I was suddenly mortified, too.

"Ahem! Ladies?" Ms. Halvorson stood over us. I felt my cheeks get as hot as a number-one single. "If

you'd like to hold it until after class, we've got an appointment here with a Mr. Charles Dickens. I think he'll provide you with plenty of drama and excitement, if that's what you're looking for."

I quickly took my seat and tried to focus my attention on *Great Expectations*. Ms. Halvorson wasn't kidding about the drama and excitement in that book. Convicts, criminals, crazy old ladies in ancient, tattered wedding dresses . . . Normally, English was my best subject. But today, I barely heard a word of the discussion.

Lisa was outta there as soon as the bell rang. I saw her grab her bag and bolt like a steel door lock. She didn't give me a second to say anything. I gathered up my books and stuffed them back into my knapsack. Minus the diary. I didn't try to catch up to her. I wasn't even sure what I would have said if she'd given me the chance.

"I just saw your friend, Lisa, race by here," Jack informed me. He was waiting for me when I got out of class. "Looked like she was training for the hundred-yard dash." His words were breezy enough, but I heard something serious in his voice.

I took a long, deep breath. "Yeah. She, um, had something to do before gym," I said lamely. Like

hole up in a quiet corner and scribble away in her newly reclaimed diary about what a jerk her best friend was. Correction: her ex-best friend.

Jack was studying me with those killer gray eyes with the gold flecks. I got the feeling he was waiting for me to say something else. Should I tell him what was going on with Lisa? What would he think? On the one hand, Lisa was being bullheaded and impossible. On the other, I knew I'd been a jerk. And I didn't want Jack to think I was one, too.

"I . . . well, Lisa and I . . ." My voice trailed off. Lisa and I what? I wasn't even sure myself what was going down.

Jack was quiet, waiting patiently for me to go on.

"Hello, you guys!" Suddenly, Liv was gliding up next to us, and the moment was shattered. "I'm not interrupting anything here, am I?"

"Oh, hey, Liv," I said, mostly relieved at being spared my confession. I was also just a teensy bit impressed at myself that Liv Magnuson and I were on an "oh, hey" basis with each other.

"I'm glad I found you," Liv said brightly. "I wanted to ask you what you're doing later."

I waited for Jack to answer. I mean, Liv and I

might be all "oh, hey," but I knew who the question was really intended for.

Jack raised his shoulders. "Hadn't thought about it," he said offhandedly. "I just hope getting home's a little less . . . exciting than the trip here," he added.

Liv gave a silvery laugh. "Well, listen, a bunch of us are going over to Pepe's for a pizza after school. You guys could hitch a ride with us. Josh's brother's picking us up in his van. I mean, I think you've had enough bus drama for one day, right?"

"You could say that," Jack agreed. He turned to me. "What do you think, Brittany?"

I thought Lisa would probably kill me. But hey, she was furious at me anyway. And I was pretty irritated with her. I looked at Jack. And at Liv. "Sure," I said, as if I went out for pizza with Liv and company all the time.

"Great," Liv said. "I'll walk with you guys to gym."

It was war on the girls' side of the gym. The dodgeball flew back and forth across the high-ceilinged room like cannon fire, accompanied by shouts and clapping and the periodic squeak of

rubber-soled gym shoes on the polyurethaned wood floor. Now, most people will tell you that dodgeball's not a real sport. That it's for wimps. I mean, you don't see it being played on TV on the *X-treme Zone*. And you won't see superbly conditioned Olympic athletes hurling a dodgeball at one another for the pride of team and country. But the way we played it at Bradford Junior High, it was serious stuff.

This game of dodgeball was for real.

We piled out of the locker room and into the gym in our navy-blue gym suits. The whole eighth grade had gym at the same time — girls on one side of the wall divider, guys on the other. Lisa was giving me the old freeze-out, and I have to admit it felt deeply bad. But I was talking and laughing with Liv and them, and trying to pretend that everything was fine.

And Lisa was talking and laughing with Sarah P. and doing the same.

Ms. Anteles, standing at ground zero in the center of the gym, gave a shrill blast on her whistle. It echoed off the walls. Ms. Anteles is short and compact, but every inch of her is steel-hard muscle. She wears black lace-up combat boots, camouflage shorts, and a Navy Seal cap over her spiky blond

46

hair. You won't catch her in something as laughable as a gym suit. We fell completely silent at the whistle.

"Listen up, people!" she roared. "The name of the game is dodgeball. No hits above the shoulders. Everything else goes. You get hit, you're out of the game. Winner is the team with the last woman standing. Choosing up sides — Hoffman, over there, O'Rourke, other side."

Lynn Hoffman and Samantha O'Rourke took their stands on opposite ends of the gym, and each chose the first girl for her team. The popular girls were chosen first, along with the good athletes, like Val Washington (starting center of the girls' basketball team) and Jeannie Pirandello (Massachusetts's junior all-around track star). Me, I'm not bad at dodgeball. Lynn picked me pretty early on, encouraged by Liv and Jane, who were already on her team.

Normally, I'd try to get Lisa on our side, but not today. I left the choosing to the other girls, and Samantha picked Lisa about halfway through the choose. Lisa said something to Sam, and they called Sarah P. over to their side.

Fine, I told myself, but I could feel my anger simmering.

Carnie Bryson was chosen dead last. Head down, she shuffled over to the other side. "Fourth-hand gym suit, anyone?" Jane said. Everybody laughed. I laughed because everyone else was laughing. Then I stopped, because let's face it — Lisa and I don't go out of our way to be nice to Carnie, but we're not cruel to her, either. I looked across the room at Lisa. She was standing at the edge of the crowd of girls on her team, and she was looking at me, too, her mouth set in a hard line.

And then I didn't have time to worry about it, because Anteles was blasting her whistle again, and the ball was in motion and coming right at me. I dodged.

A few throws later, Jane recovered the ball and launched it full force at Carnie. I watched the ball shoot across the room. Carnie was watching it, too — expressionless, uninterested. She didn't move a muscle. It slammed her right in the thigh. She flinched, but barely. Without showing any emotion, she moved out of bounds and sat down with her back against the wall of the gym.

"F for ef-fort!" Ms. Anteles yelled.

I swallowed hard. I'd seen Carnie move like lightning when it mattered to that little boy. And who

could blame her for opting out of our little war with the dodgeball?

I was so busy thinking about Carnie — and staring at her — that I didn't see the ball flying at me until it was too late. "Brittany!" someone on my team yelled, and I looked over and that thing was coming straight for me. I ducked. Just in time for the ball to make solid contact with my face.

"Ooww!" I screamed. I fell backward, bringing my hands up to my throbbing nose. They came away bloody. SCREE! The whistle blew. My teammates ran and gathered around me.

"Oh, my god, her nose!" Liv cried. "You broke it!"

I touched my nose and gingerly wobbled it back and forth. It hurt, but I didn't think it was broken. "I don't think so," I said weakly.

Anteles's whistle sounded again. "Williams! Penalty! Face throw. You're outta the game."

Williams!!? I sat up abruptly, and felt the blood rush to my nose again. As in Lisa Williams!? I searched for her across the room and spotted her staring at me in horror.

"I didn't mean to," she said to Ms. Anteles. "I mean . . . well, I was aiming at her, but below the

49

shoulders. She ducked right into the path of the ball!"

Lisa had thrown that ball? The metallic taste of blood flowed into my mouth, but that was the least of it.

So that's how we both ended up sitting on the sidelines, several yards away from Carnie — me with a tissue pressed against my nose. We watched the dodgeball fly for a few wordless, incredibly uncomfortable minutes. "Brit, I didn't mean to hurt you," Lisa finally said.

I took the tissue off for a moment, folded it in half, and reapplied it. "It did hurt," I said, without looking at her. "It hurt a lot. And I think maybe you kind of did mean to hurt me."

"Well . . . it hurt a lot to have you dump me." I could hear a quiver in Lisa's voice.

"Me? Dump you?" I turned and looked at her. "You're the one who's mad because I was in a bus accident and I couldn't give out those all-important leaflets."

Lisa closed her eyes for a moment. Then she opened them. When she spoke, her voice was soft and teary. "You know, I could understand you wanting to get to know that guy Jack. I mean, look at him. Who wouldn't? And I don't resent you for

it. Not at all. But suddenly you're hanging out with Liv and them? Brittany, you used to be so clued in to what was real. I thought you thought those girls were these huge fakes. I thought *we* thought that."

It was true. We had thought that. But that was before I'd had a chance to *be* one of those girls. All of a sudden, *I* was the big phony. "They're not so bad," I said lamely. And that was true, too. They could be fun and funny and it wasn't so awful hanging out with them. Of course, I didn't exactly feel a deep, enduring bond with any of them, either.

"Not so bad? Maybe you should ask Carnage over there if they're not so bad," Lisa commented, lowering her voice.

"Her name's Carnie," I said.

"Please. Spare me the Saint Brittany. I saw you all laughing at her," Lisa retorted.

"Oh, so now she's your best friend?" I shot back.

Lisa held my gaze in her gaze. There were unshed tears in her eyes. "Well, the position's open," she said sadly.

I felt my own eyes grow moist. Maybe I deserved it. We watched the rest of the dodgeball game in silence. My team won. Big whoop. But I had lost, and I knew it.

Chapter 7

Jack was waiting for me by the lockers, as arranged. He had that post-workout, fresh-from-the-shower glow. But it was hard for me to fully appreciate his cuteness at that moment. Lisa had really gotten to me, and nothing else came close. Not even my new and major crush.

"Brittany! What happened!?" he asked.

I was still holding a bloody tissue to my nose. "I got hit," I said, my eyes welling up.

His eyes opened wide. "Wow! You girls play rough."

"I mean by the ball. I got hit by the dodgeball," I explained. Suddenly, without warning, a tear broke free. And another.

"Hey, it'll be okay," Jack said, reaching out and touching my arm. "It's not broken, is it?"

I shook my head. Here was the cutest guy in the whole school touching the arm of yours truly . . . but the tears kept falling. I just couldn't get Lisa's

sad, hurt expression out of my mind. "That's not it. . . . It's not my nose. I mean, it's . . . well . . . my friend Lisa?"

Jack nodded. He didn't seem surprised. "Lisa. What about her? She seems nice."

"She is. Was. I mean . . . I don't know." It seemed pointless to try to explain. Why bother? Lisa had fired me from being her best friend, hadn't she? I wiped hard at the tears with my mangled tissue. "Look. It doesn't matter. So . . . you still up for pizza?" I made my voice as bright as I could. "I told Liv we'd meet her outside."

"Brittany." I could see Jack take a long breath. "I've been kind of wanting to say something all day, but I've been a little . . . I don't know . . ."

I felt even worse all of a sudden. What was he going to say? That he wanted to go to pizza with Liv alone? That he knew I was just tagging along? How much more awful could this afternoon get? "Just say it," I told him. I steeled myself.

He nodded. "Before I got here . . . well, stop me if I'm wrong, but I kinda feel you weren't all that tight with Liv and them."

I knew it. He *did* think I was a tagalong. I bristled. "Well, we've been in school together for three years. I think that qualifies as knowing each other."

"But you don't really hang with them."

I shrugged. "Maybe not before, but . . . so what?"

Jack frowned. "They don't seem like your type."

Elevator going way, way down. Subbasement. I wasn't cool enough. Or beautiful enough. I wasn't all that. And Jack knew it. "You mean, because they've, like, never had a bad hair day? Or a zit? Because they're so together? And I'm so . . . falling apart?"

Jack shook his head. "Brittany, it's true, you're not like them. They're so . . . shallow. There. I said it. Full of themselves. And you're not." I noticed his cheeks got even pinker as he said that.

I felt an instant surge of happiness. "I'm not?"

He shook his head. "Of course not. And it does matter if something's up with you and Lisa. I mean, it would matter to me . . . if I had someone who'd been my best friend for as long as you guys have been." Jack stashed his sneakers in his new locker and pushed the metal door shut. "Know why it seems kind of cool to me to stay in one place for a while? Not move around so much? It's not because I don't like the excitement. I'm really into seeing new places, having new experiences. Meeting new people." He gave me this significant look when he

said that. Now I was blushing, too. "The thing is, I meet people I really like and I have to leave them behind," Jack finished softly.

Oh, my gosh, Jack was even more amazing than I'd realized. I felt kind of swoony and light-headed. But as much as I wanted to stand here until the end of time and just drown in his gray eyes with the gold flecks, I had something to do. He'd helped me see that. "You are so totally right," I told him. "Would you . . . excuse me?"

He nodded.

I had a hard time walking away from him. I mean, how often do you bail on a chance to have pizza with a totally awesome guy? And I mean totally, totally.

Lisa wasn't in the library. She wasn't handing out Clean Harbor information on the steps of school. The last place I looked for her was the girls' bathroom.

The second my platforms hit the linoleum tiled floor, I regretted it. There were Liv and Carole, brushing their hair at the mirror. And Natalia and Jane, sitting up on the window ledge, hanging. And there was Carnie Bryson, at the sink and clearly trying to ignore them.

They all turned as I walked in. All except Carnie, who quickly pulled down a piece of paper towel and perfunctorily dried her hands. "Brit!" Liv greeted me. "Just in time to witness a one-time miracle. Carnage here was actually washing up!"

Carnie tried to leave the room, but Jane stepped in front of her. "Where are you going? Aren't you going to fix your hair, like Liv and Carole there? Or don't you own a hairbrush?"

"Lemme out," Carnie said gruffly.

"But we so rarely get the pleasure of watching you do your toiletries," Jane goaded her. "And I do mean toilet, Carnage."

"Carnie," I said.

They all looked at me. "Excuse me?" Jane asked.

"Her name is Carnie," I repeated.

"Oh. Carnie, Carnage."

"Leave her alone," I said. "All of you."

Carole raised a perfectly shaped strawberry-blond eyebrow. "Who, me? I was just brushing my hair."

"What do you care what we call her, Brittany?" Liv asked. I noticed I was no longer Brit for short.

"You know, maybe you'd be a little nicer to her

56

if you'd seen her at the bus today," I said. "I did. Right out my window. *She* was the mystery hero. If she hadn't pulled that little boy out of the way, he could have been killed!"

"No way," Natalia said. "Her? The one who helped the boy? Carnage, a hero? I didn't see her out of any window."

"You were sitting on the other side," I said.

"Brittany." Liv took a step toward me. She pointed her hairbrush at Carnie. "This is a person who smokes and cuts classes. Her brother is in jail, and if you ask me, whatever put him there runs in the family."

I couldn't believe I'd been so proud of sitting at lunch with girls like these. "You know what, Liv? That's Carnie's business, not yours," I said.

Suddenly, one of the stall doors opened. "You tell them," I heard a familiar voice say. A split second later, Lisa emerged. "Liv, why don't you and your coven go throw another eye of newt in your cauldron," she said, indicating Natalia and Carole and Jane as well.

Whoa! I blinked hard. It looked like Lisa. It sounded like Lisa. But it was totally un-Lisa-like to come charging with her guns out like that. I knew it

took every bit of guts and courage. I smiled at her. She smiled back.

"Well, Brittany," Liv harrumphed. "Maybe you'd rather hang out after school with *those* two."

I laughed. A real laugh. The first real laugh of the day. "Maybe I would," I said.

"Fine," she answered. "Come on, girls. Let's leave the B.O. trio alone. In the bathroom. Where they belong. The odor in here is just way too strong for me."

"Bye," I said sticky-sweetly. "Don't cast too many evil spells." I watched the four of them flounce out.

Carnie eyed me. Up close, I could see she wasn't dirty or smelly at all. Maybe just hardened — older-looking than thirteen, somehow. Her clothes were threadbare but clean. They hung on her as if they belonged to someone else. "Thanks," she said.

"You're welcome," I replied. "That was an incredibly good deed you did this morning."

She shrugged. "Whatever. I mean, he could have been killed. Like you said . . ."

"Why didn't you tell anyone? I mean, about what you did?" Lisa asked.

Carnie looked uncomfortable. "I get enough attention." She gazed at the door where Liv and company had exited. "And it's not fun. Besides, no

one would believe it. I probably would have ended up getting in trouble somehow."

I thought about how I'd wondered at first if Carnie had pushed the little boy. I was deeply ashamed of myself.

"Well, thanks again," Carnie said. She headed for the door. "By the way," she added, just before she walked out, "my brother's not in jail, and I don't smoke. I skip school sometimes. But, I mean, wouldn't you?" And then she was outta there.

Lisa and I stared after her. "Yeah, I guess I would," I said softly. "If people were that mean to me."

"Hey," Lisa said. "*You* weren't mean."

I was suddenly hyperaware that it was just the two of us. I flashed Lisa an embarrassed little smile. She flashed one back. "How's your nose?"

"Okay. Hurts a little, but it's stopped bleeding."

Lisa nodded. We just stood there for a moment. "Listen . . ." we both began in unison. "No, go ahead . . ." we chorused.

I gave a tentative laugh. "Wanna talk somewhere a little . . . less private?"

Lisa laughed shyly, too. "Good idea."

"I . . . well, I had it in my head to go for pizza after school," I said. Liv and them didn't own the key to Pepe's.

"Bacon and onion — make the bacon crisp?" Lisa asked.

"The only way," I agreed.

The air was sweet from all the rain, and the ground was damp. But the sun had burst through the clouds, casting a glow on the first red and orange leaves of fall.

Lisa and I ambled across the school lawn. "Lis, I'm totally, totally sorry about lunch," I said. "I'm not sure I can really explain what happened, but it's like I saw Liv waving me over to her table, and all of a sudden I thought I had won an Oscar for best new star of Bradford Junior High, you know? It was stupid. Really stupid."

"Forgiven," Lisa said simply. "If you forgive me for going off on you about my diary. I would have been a lot madder at you if you *had* read it."

I kicked at a twig on the ground. "Wait a minute. You mean you were going to be mad whether I read it or not?"

Lisa gave a little laugh. "Something like that. I guess it wasn't so much about the diary. It was more, does she care or doesn't she? Are we friends or aren't we?"

"We are," I said. "If you want to be, I mean."

Lisa stopped walking. "I want to be if you want to be."

"Wait, didn't I just say that?" I asked. "You get the feeling we're stealing each other's lines here?"

Lisa laughed. "What are best friends for?"

"Exactly," I said. And then I gave her a big, best-friend hug.

"I missed you," she said.

"Me too," I replied.

"Lis?"

"Yeah?"

"Even if we don't always agree on stuff . . . even if sometimes we want to spend our time a little differently . . . you'll always be my best friend, okay?"

"Same," Lisa said. "Totally, totally." We turned down Chestnut Street and toward town. "Hey, look." Lisa pointed down the block. I recognized him instantly, even from the back. You know how that'll happen when you're crushing on someone in a big way. "Isn't that —"

"Jack!" I called out.

He stopped and turned. He waved and waited for us to catch up with him. "Hey," he said. He looked at me and gave his lopsided smile. I knew he was glad I'd made up with Lisa.

"Hey," I echoed. "Where're you headed?"

Jack shrugged. "I didn't really feel like taking the school bus home. I've had enough thrills and action for one day, you know? So I thought I'd walk through town, check things out."

"I hear you about the school bus," I said. "Actually, we were on our way to do damage to a pizza."

"Sounds good," Jack said. "Mind if I crash your party?"

Mind? Of course I didn't mind. I opened my mouth to tell him, but then I thought better. I looked at Lisa.

She smiled shyly. "Sure," she said. "That would be nice."

We started walking. The three of us. "You know, you might not believe this, but Bradford has the best pizza outside of Italy," I informed him. "Thin crust. Nice and crisp. They have a real brick oven."

"They make a mean tomato sauce, too," Lisa said.

Jack laughed. "You know, they say the same thing in California and New Mexico and Ohio."

"Ohio? No way," I said. "Ours is the best."

But even if it wasn't, the company couldn't be beat.